STAR TREK
VOYAGER

ECHOES

**Dean Wesley Smith
Kristine Kathryn Rusch
Nina Kiriki Hoffman**

POCKET BOOKS
New York   London   Toronto   Sydney   Tokyo   Singapore

This book is a work of fiction. Names, characters, places and incidents are products of the author's imagination or are used fictitiously. Any resemblance to actual events or locales or persons living or dead is entirely coincidental.

An *Original* Publication of POCKET BOOKS

POCKET BOOKS, a division of Simon & Schuster Inc.
1230 Avenue of the Americas, New York, NY 10020

This book is published by Pocket Books, a division of
Simon & Schuster Inc., under exclusive license from
Paramount Pictures.

ISBN: 0-671-00200-7

First Pocket Books printing January 1998

10 9 8 7 6 5 4 3 2 1

POCKET and colophon are registered trademarks of
Simon & Schuster Inc.

Printed in the U.S.A.

PROLOGUE

Time: The first shift
Location: 2,410 parallel universes to the right
of ours

IT WAS A STANDARD YELLOW G-TYPE STAR SYSTEM, with thirteen planets and three dozen-odd moons. Where the fifth planet had been, a ring of asteroids slowly spread out around the sun. Some unknown event thousands of years before had destroyed the planet in that orbit. The sixth planet held the beginnings of basic life, but nothing in this system promised a humanoid civilization any time in the coming centuries.

Suddenly, a planet-sized sphere formed in the orbit where the fifth planet used to be, as if a ghost planet had come into being. It existed for seconds, then vanished.

The shape of the planet remained faint in the dark of space, however, outlined by humanoid life forms in their last struggle to breathe in the cold vacuum of space.

Three and a half billion humanoid bodies were

suddenly there in the cold of space where a planet had once existed.

Soon they were all dead, a sphere of bodies slowly moving in three and a half billion directions.

Time: The second shift
Location: 2,410 parallel universes to the right
of ours

Two and a half hours later, three and a half billion more humanoids suddenly appeared in space in the shape of the ghost planet. They floated among the dead from the shift before, struggling to survive in the cold of space.

They quickly died.

Time: The third shift
Location: 2,410 parallel universes to the right
of ours

Two and a half hours later, another three and a half billion humanoids died in the unforgiving cold of space, floating among the dead from before.

Time: The fourth through eighty-seventh shifts
Location: 2,410 parallel universes to the right
of ours

Billions of bodies floated in the shape of the ghost planet as the emptiness of space continued to fill with the grotesque shapes of death. Over and over, every two and a half hours, the unimaginable became real, as an entire population of a planet died.

Time: The first shift
Location: 2,542 parallel universes to the right
 of ours

In the east, the sky paled. Globes of light hovering above the walkways dimmed in anticipation of dawn. Cleaning machines scuttled across pale lavender pavement to polish off a few last stains before ducking into their daytime niches under the curbs. Engines hummed beneath the transportation depot.

A turquoise bird flew from one pocket green zone to another, calling, its song echoing in the spaces between low-shouldered, rounded buildings.

Lights winked and shimmered behind polarized glass walls as people rose, cleaned sleep from their systems, and prepared their morning meals.

A woman stood beside a rooftop aviary, feeding her messenger birds and wondering who would enlist her services today to send love and greetings and congratulations to special people in their lives. She lifted her head to sniff the freshening breeze: spicebark tea being brewed all over the city; the pleasurable, inviting scent of a flower to a pollinator in a nearby green zone; a faint decaying food scent from the waste collector below as it finished its rounds; and even fainter, the taste of rain and change.

A young man who had been studying all night strolled the walkway to the green zone nearest the college compartments, dodging the cleaners. He worked through an engineering problem again and again on his handheld computer, trying to figure out where his calculations had gone astray. He could not get the numbers to behave.

An old woman in another green zone sat on grass near a flowerbed and warmed her hands around a tea bulb as she watched bright-eye flowers unfold their petals in response to dawn.

Children in thousands of family complexes woke in their sleepnests, emerged, and dressed, ready for breakfast and the walk to their nearest socialization center.

Farm supervisors and weather workers yawned over spicebark tea and gathered what they needed for the day before heading for transport that would take them to outlying areas for their day's work. Others who planned to travel between cities or continents headed for the central transportation depot as well. Merchants and administrators, cooks and teachers, city engineers and scientists readied for their jobs, thinking about the latest newsbeams they had received as they rose from sleep.

Suddenly the deep blue of the morning sky filled with an intense white light that shimmered and grew brighter as each second passed. People on the walkways stopped to stare. Inside the glass-walled buildings, some cycled their glass darker to cut the glare, and others waited as the light intensified, wondering what was happening.

The engineering student in the park stilled, his computer forgotten, his mouth open as he stared at the sky.

The old woman watching the flowers looked up as well, moaning as the flowers she had been watching lost their petals in the onslaught of brightness.

The light increased until every shadow was gone and the color of every building, every tree, every blade of grass was bleached white. All details washed away on the tide of light.

Then the sky crackled, and with a slight rumbling, everything returned to normal suddenly, the intense white light gone.

And with it every person on the planet.

Gone.

Only the city remained, now empty.

Elevators stopped at the floors they had been programmed for, discharging no one.

Meals finished preparing themselves and waited uneaten in their dispenser slots.

Alarm chirps in sleepnests sounded and no one shut them off.

Showers ran ceaselessly, their cascades of water uninterrupted by humanoid forms.

Automated newscasts beamed to home screens no one watched. Live broadcasts showed empty chairs, empty desks, silent scenes.

Cleaning and maintenance machinery, sensing the absence of people, emerged from resting phase and went to work.

On a rooftop, messenger birds flew out through the open aviary door and circled in the sky, wings edged in early sunlight. Their message cavities were empty, their guidance nodes inactive.

A few automatic sirens went off.

Otherwise, the city was quiet.

And empty.

CHAPTER
1

Time: The eighty-seventh shift
Location: Our universe

CAPTAIN KATHRYN JANEWAY GLANCED UP FROM THE screen of her book padd at the stars out the viewports of the ready room. Something had jarred her out of a fictional early nineteenth-century world back into the twenty-fourth century.

She had tired of reading about gloomy governesses in remote mansions on the moors, and was sampling a period piece with a different flavor, a comedy of manners set during the British Regency, Earthdate 1816, though written a century later. In her off-duty hours she enjoyed reading about stratified, rigid societies where people behaved according to outmoded codes.

Not that she had many off-duty hours these days. Off-duty minutes seemed more like it. The warp engines had failed a week before, and she and B'Elanna had been putting in long hours getting them back on-line. Then a personnel crisis had erupted among the junior engineering staff. Normally, she would have let B'Elanna handle it, but Klingons—even half-Klingons—had notoriously foul moods when they were sleep-deprived. Chakotay had tried to settle it, but his usual low-key style had failed. Janeway had stepped in, using the last of her energy and all of her diplomatic skills. The crisis had passed, but it had taken her reserves with it.

Both Chakotay and Tuvok had hinted that she needed rest. This afternoon, she took their advice, but she couldn't bring herself to take the entire afternoon off. She had too much work to catch up on. She didn't have time for her favorite holodeck program, so she picked up an old novel instead.

She liked books. A real book could be read in snatches, seconds of escape and relaxation, instead of an afternoon's worth. Sometimes seconds were all she had.

But in those seconds, she could disappear into a good book. And this book was good. She wasn't certain what jarred her out of it.

She scanned her ready room.

The stars looked normal, the long streaks of light that always appeared when the ship was traveling at warp six. She shifted on the couch and glanced toward her computer console, where she had left her commbadge, wondering if someone had hailed her.

Silence.

No. If someone had hailed her, she would have reacted instantly. What had startled her?

A faint shudder vibrated through her. She felt

the movement coming up through the couch. She glanced at the glass bowl of yellow-green star lilies on the round table nearby. The flowers had come from Kes's wonderful gardens in airponics that morning—another gift she had left them. Fresh flowers in the ready room were part of Neelix's morale strategy.

The water wavered inside the clear glass. Ripples ringed the stems of the flowers.

With the touch of her finger, Janeway marked her place and slept her book padd.

This was what had disturbed her, this shudder.

Smoothing her uniform, she got to her feet. Everything in the ready room appeared normal. Illuminated artwork hung straight on the walls, and her bottle and memento shelves looked undisturbed. Her mobile work chair near the computer console had not shifted a centimeter.

She felt another shuddering bump through the floor.

Whatever this was, she could feel it through the whole ship. And that worried her. Anything that could affect the entire *Voyager* was too important to be ignored.

Even though Chakotay hadn't deemed this phenomenon important enough to interrupt her off-duty time, she had to know what was going on.

Janeway paused when she stepped onto the bridge.

Panels and consoles glowed with flickering colors in the half-light. Data streams, ship schematics, starmaps, and lighted touch-control panels blinked normally. The sound and feel of engines and systems hummed all through *Voyager*. She hadn't felt an odd vibration since she left the ready room.

The large forward viewscreen displayed the long, colored chalk marks of star systems passing to either side of *Voyager*'s route. She heard the beeps and peeps on controls as they responded to her crew's manipulations. The smell of people and uniforms and power and ship's metal welcomed her. There was no feeling of frenzy here.

Ensign Harry Kim frowned at his console. Commander Chakotay leaned forward in the command chair, alert, and Lieutenant Tom Paris, at the helm, glanced from the viewscreen to Kim and back. Lieutenant Commander Tuvok stood at his station, his dark brows lowered. Ensign Julie Starr studied ship status arrays.

On this routine leg of the journey, the bridge crew was down to half strength.

"Commander," Janeway said as she made her way to the command chair. "What are these vibrations?"

Chakotay stood the moment he saw her. "Subspace waves, Captain. They're very weak. I thought I would investigate before disturbing you."

"I'm not that tired, Chakotay," she said, even though she appreciated his concern. She had been working very hard these last few weeks. Both Chakotay and Tuvok had made a point of mentioning it to her. And now, it seemed, they had conspired to give her more time away from the bridge.

She would stop the coddling immediately. The next time one of them told her she needed a rest, she would remind him, quite sharply, that only she and the doctor could determine the state of her health.

"You should have called me to the bridge as soon as you felt them," she said.

"My mistake, Captain," Chakotay said.

"Have you pinpointed the source of these waves?" Janeway asked as she took the command chair. Chakotay moved to his normal place beside her.

"Mr. Tuvok?" Chakotay asked.

"The waves appear to be spherical in nature," Tuvok said. "I will have their point of origin in one-point-two minutes."

"Spherical?" Janeway asked. "As if someone tossed a stone into a puddle of water?"

"It is more complicated than that, Captain," Tuvok said. "It—"

"But the analogy does work," Ensign Kim said. Janeway smiled at him. He was becoming good at forestalling Tuvok's long, unnecessary explanations.

Tuvok stared at his screen. "I have pinpointed the origin, Captain. The waves emanate from a system thirty light-years away from us."

"What kind of transmissions are these?"

"Unclear, Captain. The energy signatures match nothing in our database." Tuvok sounded puzzled.

Janeway activated her own science screen and called up the information on it. She didn't recognize the signatures either. "Mr. Kim, I want you to see if these are carrier waves or data transmissions. Analyze these waves using the ship's language database. See if the universal translator can make sense of it, if all else fails."

"Maybe it's some kind of weapon," Paris said.

"Doubtful, Mr. Paris," Tuvok said. "There are more effective ways to use weapons in space."

"Actually, Tuvok," Janeway said, "Mr. Paris has a good point. This effect may be caused by a weapon we're unfamiliar with."

She examined her screen more closely and found that the wave still eluded her.

"Will these waves affect the ship?" Chakotay asked.

"No, sir," Kim said. "Our shields will protect us."

"But how far?" Chakotay asked. "Can we get closer to the cause of this thing?"

"Yes," Tuvok said. "The shields would protect us even if we were at the point of origin."

"At the point of origin," Janeway repeated. She shoved her screen away. "Tuvok, how far off course would we have to go to investigate this disturbance?"

"Two-point-six light-years," Tuvok said. "But it might be dangerous. The pattern and regularity of the waves suggest that the disturbance is artificial. A civilization that has the power to create such regular subspace waves must have a highly advanced technology."

Janeway sighed. Much as she loved investigating

new things, she knew better than to veer off course to satisfy her own curiosity. "Monitor the situation, Chakotay," she said as she stood. "See if you can discover from this distance what's causing those waves. And let me know if they get worse."

"Aye, Captain," Chakotay said, although he made no move to resume the command chair.

"I'll be in my ready room." The novel no longer sounded exciting to her. She loved discovery, loved to explore each nook and cranny of the universe. Which gave her an idea. She stopped and turned around. "Tuvok, filter any information you gather into my computer."

She ignored the slight shaking of Chakotay's head. She would investigate from there. It would, in its own way, be as relaxing as the novel. And she did need the relaxation. Much as she disliked Tuvok and Chakotay's heavy-handed reminders, they had a point. She hadn't been sleeping more than four hours a night since the warp engines went off-line a week ago. She had enjoyed the work, but not the following personnel crisis. Those things always put her teeth on edge, and interrupted her sleep.

"Captain." Kim's voice had a touch of surprise in it. "I'm getting a faint distress signal."

"From where, Mr. Kim?"

"The same place those waves are coming from."

"Well," Janeway said, moving back to face the main screen. "That clearly means the waves aren't some form of communication. You're certain you're getting a distress signal?"

"Absolutely, Captain."

She didn't like the thread of anticipation that ran through her. Her curiosity had been aroused more than she expected it to be. "Well, then, Mr. Kim, it seems we have an invitation. Mr. Paris, set a course for that system. Let's see who needs our help."

CHAPTER 2

Time: The eighty-seventh ~~shift~~
Location: Our universe

THE SUBSPACE WAVES WERE DISQUIETING. JANEWAY leaned forward as another vibrated through the ship. Nothing harmful happened, yet the wave felt somehow *wrong*. She wasn't certain if that was because subspace waves had, in the past, been indicators of disasters, or if it was because she was so attuned to *Voyager* that the least little difference set her teeth ajar.

Probably a combination of both.

And neither.

Sometimes she had a sense, a mild sense, of things that were about to happen. Mark used to say she was so attuned to the world around her that she could pinpoint the cause and the effect of any difference, giving her a slight prescience. She preferred to think of it as an edge. An instructor of hers at the Academy said that all leaders had such an edge. It was a way of thinking about the details of a situation that marked a successful leader.

The instructor believed it was a skill that could be taught and developed.

He had certainly instilled it in Janeway, if she hadn't had the ability already.

"Captain, we're approaching the planet where the waves originate." Paris gave her the information as he took them out of warp.

"On screen," she said.

From the angle *Voyager* approached the planet, half of it lay in darkness. In the forward viewscreen, Janeway studied the spots of yellow and orange light along the eastern seaboard of one of the larger continents in the southern hemisphere.

Cities.

"The distress signal, Mr. Kim?" she asked.

"We're still receiving it," he said. "It hasn't changed. It seems to be automated."

Nothing looked out of place. The atmosphere-softened crescent planet glowed deep-sea blue beneath a few scarves and tatters of brilliant white clouds, with a desert-banded continent and a string of green islands just coming into view around the dayside curve of the horizon. Though the continental shapes were different from those of Earth, the greens and ochre of the land masses, the shades and nuances of blue in the ocean, the white swirls of an equatorial storm, the glint of the icy polar caps were so similar that she could almost imagine she was coming home, that somewhere below Mark and her dog, Molly Malone, waited to greet her.

She wondered if she would ever get over that longing for Earth. It arose at the strangest times.

"Mr. Tuvok, have you located the source of those waves?"

"They are emanating from the planet, Captain."

Janeway smiled. "That's why we're here, Tuvok."

He didn't respond, but a single eyebrow rose in acknowledgment of her sarcasm. It used to baffle him so, but now he was used to it.

"Mr. Kim," Janeway said, "lock onto that distress beacon, but don't hail them yet. I want to know a bit more about this planet before we contact them."

"Aye, Captain," Kim said.

"Captain," Tuvok said, "it will take me some minutes to discover the source of those waves. I suggest contacting the surface. They will—"

"Yes, Mr. Tuvok." Janeway waved a hand. "All in good time."

She got up from her chair and went to Ensign Kim's station. "What sort of readings are you getting, Mr. Kim?"

"It looks like this is standard early-warp culture," Ensign Kim said, "with a population of nearly three and a half billion. There are a number of satellites and other celestial objects in orbit around the planet. Their energy signatures are consistent with early-warp."

"Very good," Janeway said. She had expected a bit more advanced culture. But early-warp problems were usually something that *Voyager* could handle. Warp cultures seemed to go through the same types of development, no matter how many light-years apart they were.

"Mr. Tuvok," Janeway said, "when is the next subspace pulse due?" Because they had dropped out of warp, the time between pulses had lengthened. Janeway knew Tuvok would be keeping track.

"The next pulse will hit in six minutes, five seconds, Captain," Tuvok said. "I am still searching for the cause."

"All right, Ensign," Janeway said to Kim. "I think it's time to—"

"Captain?" Lieutenant Torres's voice broke in from Engineering. She spoke rapidly, and she sounded excited.

"Go ahead," Janeway said.

"There are traces of armacolite in the structures below."

"Armacolite?" Janeway asked. She sat back in her chair. They had gone out of their way for a distress signal and encountered a bit of luck. If they had had armacolite earlier in the week, Janeway wouldn't have lost all that sleep helping Torres get the warp engines on-line.

"Yes, Captain," Torres said. "They seem to have it everywhere. Far more than enough for us to replenish our supplies."

"I have the same readings," Kim said. His voice rose with excitement as well. The entire crew knew how important this discovery was.

Armacolite was a rare and valuable mineral they needed to rebuild the Oltion Coils in their warp engines. In the Alpha Quadrant, there were plants that manufactured armacolite in several sectors, but its use was apparently not widespread in the Delta Quadrant. They had only found one source since arriving, and their dwindling supplies had been a constant worry. It had led to some rigging of the engines that made them even more sensitive than usual.

"Captain," Tuvok said. "I have still not pinpointed the cause of the disturbance."

"Captain?" Torres said, her voice nearly covering Tuvok's. "I would love to take an away team—"

"As soon as we discover the problem, B'Elanna. The armacolite will have to wait. I will contact you." Janeway signed off. "Tuvok, keep working to find that disturbance. Mr. Kim, it's time to answer that distress call."

"Aye, Captain."

She stood in the center of the bridge, and adjusted her uniform. Now their mission to this planet had a twofold purpose: She would see if she could help solve the problems the planet was having, and she would try to leave with some armacolite.

Kim worked over his console. He stared unseeing across the bridge as he listened to his ear transmitter, his hands moving over the controls. "Exploring bandwidths for—I've found their normal communications frequencies. Isolating signals. Sending hail. Receiving . . . On screen!"

An auburn-haired, brown-skinned humanoid appeared on the forward viewscreen. He looked muscular, solid, and startlingly human, right down to the deep worry grooves in his forehead. His short hair stuck up in tufts on one side of his head, as though he had just risen from sleep and hadn't had time to groom.

The curved wall behind him was green and glassy; clouds were visible through it and inset with a squiggly gridwork of yellow and darker green lines or wires. Light flickered from bits of the gridwork.

The humanoid's gray eyes widened as he stared out of the screen at them. He wore a toga-like green garment edged with narrow blue lines, and had a wide gold chain around his neck. "Greetings, stranger ship. Are you receiving? Can you understand me?" He looked down at something out of view and moved his arms. Static buzzed a moment. He glanced up again, eyebrows lifted. "Is that better?"

He certainly didn't seem panicked. But Janeway had learned long ago that different cultures handled stress differently.

She decided to ignore his questions and give him the standard greeting. It would show him that she was receiving clearly. "I'm Captain Kathryn Janeway of the Federation *Starship Voyager*. We answered your distress signal."

"Ah, wondrous!" the man said. She was beginning to feel uncomfortable. Out of the corner of her eye, she saw Chakotay shifting slightly. Tuvok had raised his head. He would say, if he could, that this man's reaction wasn't logical.

"We assumed you were in some sort of distress."

"Yes, thank you." The man clapped his hands together like a child with a new toy. "A ship of a design I've never seen, and yet we can converse. Astonishing!"

Tom Paris turned in his chair. His eyes were wide.

Janeway ignored him as best she could. She would have to assume that they were the first true aliens the man had ever seen. "We were thirty light-years away when we received your signal," she said again, thinking that if he were nonresponsive this time, she might have to explain the use of a distress signal to him.

"Thank you for responding to our beacon," he said, bobbing slightly. "I'm R'Lee, head of the World Council of Birsiba."

"A pleasure to make your acquaintance, sir," Janeway said. "What is the nature of your emergency?"

"It is quite . . . unsettling." R'Lee had stopped bobbing. His hands remained clasped together, and he pressed them against his chest. "I assume you know of the subspace waves radiating out from our planet?"

"We encountered them before we received your signal," Janeway said. "Are they the source of your distress?"

R'Lee's hands seemed to push harder against his chest. "The waves started eight days ago as we activated our worldwide transport system for the first time. We think we may have triggered some sort of subspace rift far beyond our power to handle. And now we can't turn it off."

Janeway glanced around at Tuvok. "His explanation is consistent with my findings," Tuvok said. "Although I am still unable to pinpoint the exact source."

"You can't turn off your transport system?" Janeway asked. "Or the source of the rift?"

"We believe the system *is* the source of the rift, and we cannot shut it off," R'Lee said.

"So you have no way of testing the theory," Janeway said. "Are these waves causing problems for your people?"

R'Lee's hands dropped to his sides. "Nothing of consequence," he said, "and yet it all has consequences."

"I'm afraid I don't understand," Janeway said.

R'Lee glanced down at his toga, then to the side. He leaned off screen for a moment, then lifted a cube into view. "My family," he said, displaying a holographic representation of himself, a handsome, thin woman, and a pleasant-looking large woman with her arms around the shoulders of a grinning pixieish child of indeterminate gender.

Janeway smiled and nodded, not understanding what this had to do with the waves.

R'Lee tilted the cube so he could see its image. He frowned. "Lula, our child—in every memory I have of her, her eyes are green, like her gene mother's. But here in the cube, they are gray like mine."

Janeway hoped they were having another communication difficulty. She didn't like the trivial nature of the exchange. "Surely the image is flawed."

"I have had this cube on my desk for two years," said R'Lee. "I glance at it often while I work. Always I'm comforted by the sight of my daughter, the light in her eyes. Her green eyes."

"I see," said Janeway, not seeing at all. Was this man delusional? Had they responded to a distress call because someone had had a bad dream or couldn't remember the color of his daughter's eyes? Was this a measure of how stressless this planet usually was, that the head of the World Council could ask the universe for outside help because of such a minor glitch?

"I realize this does not sound like a major problem," R'Lee said, echoing Janeway's thoughts. "A picture changing is not a large event. Few of the changes people have reported to my staff from all around the world seem major. Perhaps the color of bedding in someone's sleepnest has shifted from light blue to dark blue, or someone discovers the wrong flavor of spicebark tea in his storage compartment, or someone finds cherputa in her window herb box instead of gloven."

He frowned, glancing around as if almost embarrassed. "Taken each alone, these changes are trivial. A mere annoyance. A chance to try something new. Cumulatively, though . . . the accretion of changes following each subspace wave is alarming. Every time one of the waves pulses, some other thing is different."

Janeway took a deep breath. Little differences, all over the planet. Each time a subspace wave hits. Like the vibrations running through *Voyager*. Small, subtle, and letting her know something was wrong.

"Are these changes universal to your population?" she asked.

R'Lee frowned. "Not everyone, or every time. Sometimes everything stays the same for some people. Sometimes it changes a lot for others. Some have woken up in the wrong apartments, a few even in the wrong city or on the wrong continent." He shook his head. "Each pulse takes us farther away from the lives we knew. What will the next pulse bring?"

What indeed? Janeway suddenly understood the nature of the disturbance. A runaway system with small implications, leading, perhaps, to something larger.

But if they had caught it early enough, a small solution might be all that is needed. And if they were able to stop the waves, then R'Lee's people might be willing to part with some armacolite.

R'Lee said, "I have science teams working on this problem around the clock, and we have been unable to come up with solutions on how to shut down the transportation system. We need help!"

"We'll be glad to see what we can do," Janeway said.

"Ten seconds to the next wave," Tuvok said.

"Stand by, sir," Janeway said. "We will resume communication after the wave hits."

She signaled to Kim to shut off the communication. Then she said, "Record every piece of data you can about this pulse. If we can help them with this, we might just be able to do some trading."

"Good idea," Chakotay said.

Kim smiled, then went to work.

"I want the planet on screen," Janeway said. She turned to face it as the new image registered.

Slowly ripples formed in the upper atmosphere of the planet below, blurring the colors and the outlines of the land masses and oceans. Then the entire planet was bathed in a blinding white light.

Ensign Starr gasped. Paris put up an arm to shield his eyes from the glare.

Kim hit polarizing dampers for the viewscreen, cutting the light down to bearable levels. Janeway blinked at retinal ghosts.

Suddenly, in a strange silence, like the cessation of breath and heart, the pause between one instant and the next, everything shifted.

Instead of just one planet below, there were thousands, slightly overlapping, like beads strung on a loop, leading off to right and left in repeating, diminishing orbs away into infinity, the sort of distance visible in face-to-face mirrors.

"What . . ." Janeway said. She'd never seen anything like this before.

Above every second planet was an orbiting *Voyager,* a glinting image against the white and blue swirl of clouds over ocean. How strange, Janeway thought, to see her ship stroboscopically like this: Blink, it was there over a planet; Blink, it was gone over the next planet; Blink, and there it was again—thousands of *Voyager*s telescoping into the distance as far as Janeway could see.

But only above every *second* planet.

The sight lasted for just over three seconds, then vanished as quickly as it had come.

The ship rocked slightly from the impact of the subspace wave. Below them the planet had apparently returned to normal.

Silence filled the bridge. Janeway knew they had seen something of incredible magnitude, something her crew had never seen before.

She had wanted to explore each facet of the universe: It seemed she was getting her chance.

"Find out what that was," she said, and the crew snapped into motion.

CHAPTER 3

Time: The eighty-seventh shift
Location: 2,410 parallel universes to the right
of ours

CAPTAIN KATHRYN JANEWAY SAT IN THE COMMAND
chair, staring at the debris field in the forward
viewscreen, the apparent origin of the strange
subspace pulses *Voyager* had been experiencing at
regular intervals since they had arrived in this
sector. She twisted her head slightly. Her braid was
too tight, and when she had pulled it into its
customary crown around her head, she pulled too
hard. Now, with the debris before them, she didn't
have time to take care of the irritation.

Long-range scans had uncovered mostly myster-
ies about this dense cloud. Tuvok had already
determined that the debris field did not have the
mass of a planet, though it had a strange, almost
planetary appearance. It was compressed at the
poles but broad at the equators, and had a cohe-
siveness that was difficult to understand, given its
lack of mass. It was a strange object to find in an

asteroid belt where a fifth planet had once been; strange to find anywhere, actually, but here there was something particularly unsettling about it.

Something ghostly.

The mass of debris did not have the necessary gravity to produce the orbit or spin it was undergoing, making Janeway wonder if there was a local gravitational anomaly that would explain both the appearance of this peculiar object and the strange subspace pulses emanating from it.

At the left helm position in front of her, Tom Paris rubbed the back of his neck above his orange and black uniform jacket as he stared up at the screen. To his right, second helmsman Ensign Parvoneh studied her control panels and arrays. *Voyager* was approaching the debris field at a quarter impulse, cautiously edging closer to the source of the pulses. Commander Chakotay sat to her left, his back rigid as he surveyed the scene.

"Captain," Ensign Harry Kim said, "one minute until the next subspace pulse."

"Prepare our sensor array," Janeway said. "We need to collect data on as many spectra as possible while that pulse is being emitted."

She stared at the debris field as it slowly grew on the screen. There was something disquieting about it, and the disquiet came not just from its scientific anomaly. If she had to use an unscientific description, she would have chosen one from her North American ancestry: *A ghost walked on my grave.*

She didn't like that thought. She stood and moved up to the communication post.

"Ensign Kim, how are those spectrometric analyses of the debris field coming?" asked Janeway. They had been beyond scanning range during the most recent subspace pulse.

"Captain," Kim said softly. "I—" Then he stopped.

Janeway looked at him. His face was pale. Sweat dotted it. Then he turned green. She thought he was going to be ill. He gripped the console, his knuckles white, his gaze fixed.

"Ensign?" she asked.

He didn't seem to hear her.

"Ensign, what is it?" She used her command voice, trying to recall him to a sense of where he was and what he was doing.

"The mass . . . the sphere . . ." he managed to say, then gulped and closed his eyes. He swayed, but remained standing.

"Hold it together, Harry," Paris said. "What did you find?"

Janeway didn't mind the breach of protocol. It was more important to learn what Harry had seen than to learn it in proper fashion. Paris and Kim were friends, and Paris knew he, if anyone, could reach Kim.

But Kim, for the first time since he set foot on *Voyager,* appeared unable to answer. Whatever he had seen had bothered him so deeply he could not find the words.

Janeway moved back to her own chair, sat down, pulled up her science console, and punched in the coordinates. As she did so, she snapped, "Tuvok, tell me what these readings are. And someone see to Ensign Kim."

"Captain." Tuvok's voice sounded cold, almost strangled.

"Captain," he said slowly, his voice just barely under control, "the mass of debris in the shape of the planet is composed of organic material."

"Organic material?" Janeway asked. "Is it alive?"

"No, Captain," Tuvok said. "It comprises, in my estimate, over three hundred billion separate humanoid forms. All dead."

"Three hundred *billion?*" Janeway's mind couldn't grasp what Tuvok had just said.

Three hundred billion. That number had no meaning in her mind. She turned to face the front screen, where the dark round planet-sized mass hung in front of the ship in space.

Billions of humanoid bodies.

All floating in space in the shape of a planet.

No. That wasn't possible. It had to be a hallucination.

She glanced at her own console. Her readings came out the same way.

Her fingers shook.

She glanced at her bridge crew, her mind not grasping what was on the screen as anything possible.

Paris had closed his eyes.

Chakotay stared coldly at the screen.

Parvoneh had tears streaming down her face.

Kim was beginning to regain control. His skin

was still pale, and he seemed vaguely sick, but his dark eyes focused on her when she looked at him. In them, she saw understanding and an incomprehensible sorrow.

"I'm sorry, Captain," Kim said, his voice shaky. She wasn't sure if he was talking about his failure to respond to her earlier question, his emotional reaction, or her sudden realization of what was going on.

He knew, just as she did, that no one on the crew had ever seen this kind of slaughter before.

"Are you fit to continue duty, Ensign?" she asked, unwilling—unable—to think about the emotional ramifications of their discovery. If she did, she would have a response like Kim's, and she couldn't afford to. She needed to maintain tight control of herself in order to maintain tight control of her ship.

Until she knew what caused those deaths, and those bodies to be piled the way they were, *Voyager* herself could be in danger.

"Ensign Kim," she said again. "Are you fit?"

"Aye, Captain," he said slowly. "I'm fit."

"Good. Magnify—"

"Captain," Tuvok broke in. "Another subspace pulse is commencing."

Suddenly the mass of bodies vanished in an eye-burning flash of white light, and then the entire scene was replaced by a strange sight.

To the left, a stretch of repeating asteroid belts like the one she had seen in the viewscreen before the pulse, diminishing with distance, each second one with a *Voyager* drifting near it. There must have been at least a hundred or more asteroid belts, but she was very glad to see that there was only one mass of bodies. And that was in front of her ship and her ship only.

Only one.

In front of her ship. She didn't know what that meant. Beyond the hundred or so asteroid belt images, a shimmering string of ocean-blue, white-clouded planets, lovely as mirages or heavens, slightly overlapping, disappeared into the distance, an infinity of mirror images facing each other, limited only by the distance of vision.

To the right was another beautiful string of planets curling off into another distance.

Above every second planet was another *Voyager*. Not every planet, but every *other* planet, as if there was a gap in the reflective mirror. Janeway instantly wondered why every planet and asteroid belt didn't have a *Voyager*. If this were a trick of light somehow, how to explain the deletion?

The scene lasted for what seemed to be an eternity to Janeway, but was only a few seconds. Then space returned to normal.

"Captain!" Kim's shaky voice had recovered much of its power. "Another three and a half billion bodies have joined the mass in front of us. And—" His voice broke again for just a moment. Then he said words that Janeway found very hard to imagine.

"They're all alive."

CHAPTER 4

Time: The eighty-eighth shift
Location: Our universe

"FIND OUT WHAT THAT WAS!" JANEWAY REPEATED. Her eyes still burned from the light, from seeing the array of *Voyager*s and planets disappearing off into the distance in both directions. She still had to get back to her conversation with R'Lee, but that could wait a few moments. This anomaly was strange, startling, and as disconcerting as a hall of mirrors.

"I do not know what it was, Captain," Tuvok said. "But it registered on all of our sensors."

"As what?" she asked.

"That's hard to say, Captain," Ensign Kim said. "It happened so fast."

"Figure it out," she snapped. "That wasn't normal."

"Perhaps we are going out of phase again?" Chakotay suggested, somewhat softly.

"There's no plasma cloud this time," Paris said.

"That wasn't the entire cause of the problem the last time, Lieutenant," Tuvok said.

Janeway shuddered. She had come so close to losing *Voyager* that time. When the ship had gone out of phase with itself, it had somehow created, or met, another *Voyager* that nearly destroyed this one. Ensign Kim was actually a refugee from that *Voyager*.

"Is that what's going on here?" she asked Kim.

"The readings are completely different, Captain," he said.

"Yes, but what are those readings saying?"

Kim looked at her over the console, his dark eyes sincere. "Right now, they're reading the same way they did when we arrived. We've just come through a subspace pulse."

"Do we know what caused the pulse?"

"No," Tuvok said. "But we saw all the other *Voyager*s inside the pulse, in a manner of speaking."

"The other *Voyager*s," Janeway said, "and more planets. Ensign, put me back in touch with R'Lee."

"Yes, Captain."

The screen switched from its view of the planet to a view of R'Lee. He had changed clothes. His toga was blue now, and he wore a silver chain around his neck.

What an odd thing to do in the middle of a crisis. But his reactions had been odd thus far anyway.

"R'Lee," Janeway said. "During that last subspace pulse, did you get a duplication effect, rather like looking into a series of reflections?"

R'Lee was staring at her with stunned amazement.

34

"You are a being from another place?" he asked.

"We've been through this, R'Lee. That last pulse created a strange effect here. I need to know if it was duplicated below."

"A ship of a design I have never seen before," R'Lee said, "and yet we can converse. Astonishing!"

"R'Lee," Janeway said, "you're repeating yourself."

"Oh, wondrous one," R'Lee said, "I have never spoken these words to you. I have never before seen you. Did you receive our distress signal?"

Janeway glanced over her shoulder at Tuvok. "Yes," she said slowly. "We responded to your signal. I am Captain Kathryn Janeway, and this is the starship *Voyager.*"

"I am R'Lee," he said, "head of the World Council of Birsiba. But you seem to know that already. Your people must have great wisdom."

"No," Janeway said, "just memory of a prior conversation that you don't seem to recall." She glanced at Kim, who shrugged. She turned back to the screen. "Now, I need you to tell me what happened during that last subspace pulse. Did you get a duplication effect?"

R'Lee squinched his strange features, gamely trying to figure out what she needed. "No duplication effect, Captain. Is that how I am to address you? Captain?"

"Yes," she said. "No duplication effect. Yet you have no memory of our previous conversation?"

"None, fine lady," R'Lee said. "I am quite sure I

would recall it, as you are the first unusual being I have encountered."

"Mr. Kim," Janeway said, "has there been a time-shift here, perhaps on the planet itself?"

"No, Captain," Kim said. "I don't know what could be causing this."

"Captain, if I might have a moment," Chakotay said.

"Stand by, R'Lee," Janeway said. She signaled Kim to cut off the communication. "Yes, Chakotay?"

"During your first conversation with R'Lee, he seemed rather remote, detached."

"Much as he is now," she said with a touch of impatience. She didn't like something she didn't understand.

"And when you asked him what was wrong, he mentioned an image of his child, claiming her eyes changed color."

"His clothing has changed color," Janeway said softly. "Are you saying the subspace pulse is causing some sort of pigmentation changes on the planet?"

"No," Chakotay said. "R'Lee had enough time to change clothing. But during the pulse he forgot us, and he might have forgotten the clothing change."

"You think this is affecting his mind," Janeway said. "It is possible, I suppose."

She didn't like the theory, though. It was too simple. In the historical novels she so loved, people always believed that someone different was having mental problems.

"Captain," Kim said, "at this point we don't know what the pulse is doing. It is having a duplication effect up here. If it's having the same thing down below, only in a slightly different phase, it could interfere with biochemistry."

"Or, Captain," Tuvok said, "there is the possibility that this is the way Birsiban society works. We will not know until we investigate further."

"I was planning to send an away team," Janeway said. "Is there the possibility that this anomaly will hurt our people?"

"There is always that possibility," Tuvok said. "But I do not see any readings that would, at this point, lead me to believe that such an event will occur. Do you concur, Ensign?"

"Yeah," Kim said. "I do."

The Captain nodded once. She could send the Doctor down, but the subspace pulses had an energy base, and that might interfere with his systems. She would put Kes on the away team. Kes had medical knowledge and a clear head. She would get the team back aboard if it were a medical necessity.

"Get R'Lee," Janeway said. She braced herself, waiting for R'Lee to appear. When he did, he still wore his blue outfit and silver chain.

"Do you remember me, R'Lee?" she asked.

"But of course," he said. "Have you decided to help us? You do not yet know what the problem is. Perhaps if I explain—"

"You've already explained," Janeway said. "And we are going to help you. We'll be sending a team of our people down to investigate your transport system. I trust you'll give them all the help they need?"

"But of course, Captain. We shall bring them flowers if the need arises."

"Flowers," Janeway said dryly.

R'Lee smiled. "It is but a figure of speech."

"Colorful," Paris said under his breath. "Very colorful."

Janeway hoped that R'Lee hadn't heard him. "Our team shall arrive shortly," she said. "Janeway out." Then she turned to Paris.

He raised his hands. "I know, I know. Keep the comments to myself."

"Especially when you're below, Lieutenant. You and Commander Chakotay get Lieutenant Torres and Kes, and beam to the surface."

Chakotay and Paris stood, and prepared to leave.

"Commander," Janeway said. "A moment."

Chakotay waited. Paris glanced over his shoulder, but didn't stop as he went to the turbolift.

"Chakotay," she said. "I want you out of there if it looks like the subspace pulse will affect you."

Chakotay grinned at her. "Aye, Captain," he said. Then he turned and walked off the bridge.

As she watched him go, a shiver ran down her back. The images of *Voyager* stretching to infinity returned to her. That was one surprise too many on this trip. She hoped there wouldn't be any others.

CHAPTER 5

Time: The eighty-eighth shift
Location: 2,542 parallel universes to the right
of ours

PARIS SCUFFED HIS BOOTS ON THE PURPLE WALKWAY,
which was slick and whistle-clean and hummed
faintly under his feet. Chakotay, Torres, and Kes
were beside him, still standing in the positions they
had assumed when they got onto the transporter.
Chakotay and Torres had their tricorders out. Kes
was staring at their surroundings.

Paris stared too.

Stalagmites of translucent, many-colored glass-
sided buildings rose up all around the meandering
walkways. There were no corners or hard angles
anywhere. He could smell flowers and grass and
some spicy but unidentifiable scents, could hear
the murmur of invisible machines and a trickle of
water. This was a pretty place.

Pretty, and completely empty of the people who
had built it or lived in it. Nobody was home on the
entire planet except flora and fauna.

He could feel the emptiness. Something undefinable made it feel strange, like a room recently vacated. A whiff of a perfume, perhaps, or the fact that it was all so clean.

Paris glanced behind him toward a small emerald park. Trees and shrubs shaded grassy areas. A tiny stream ran from one edge to another, embracing rocks and slipping beneath a zigzag bridge of thick, narrow, blue-streaked clear glass slabs. Half-hidden by leafy branches, something white and molded glinted in the sunlight. A bird flew from one tree to another.

Chakotay looked up from his tricorder, a frown on his dark face. The two concentric circles tattooed on his left cheek stretched tight across his cheekbone. His vivid red and maroon uniform looked dark against the lighter colors of the city beyond him.

Gold and maroon–suited Torres directed her tricorder in a circle, studying the readings she was getting.

Kes headed toward the park, holding her hands out in the direction of the plants. Today she wore an olive green dress, with slashes of her pink undergarment visible through the upper sleeves and at the neck. "This place is so empty," she whispered. "It just feels . . . wrong."

So she felt it too. But of course she did. Kes was more in tune with the universe than Paris would ever be. And she was right about how wrong it all felt. Paris had been in abandoned places before, but they *felt* abandoned: dust-covered, disheveled, falling to ruin. They never felt like this.

This was not some wilderness or some dilapi-
dated building, but a space that should be full of
people going about their daily routines. Paris
hunched his shoulders. This was a city. There
should be people around here. Kids playing, par-
ents working, people eating, whatever people did
for fun on this planet. Somewhere there should be a
bar, maybe the local equivalent of a pool table, and
some women, whatever the local women looked
like; somebody to share a drink with.

But there wasn't a humanoid soul on the whole
planet except for the members of the away team.
Harry and Tuvok had made that clear in the
conference room earlier. Scans had revealed a
planet full of evidence of civilization and empty of
inhabitants. The energy signatures of machines
showed that the planet was still powered up and
running.

Where had all the people gone?

It was as if everyone had stepped out to get a nice
breakfast and had never come back.

Creepy.

"Strange things happen in this sector, Captain,"
Neelix had said at the meeting.

"Strange things, Mr. Neelix?" the Captain had
asked. "What sorts of strange things?"

"I don't know," he had said, looking away. "This
was a bit out of my range. I'd heard, though, of
ships disappearing and hostiles nearby."

"We have seen no evidence of hostiles, Mr.
Neelix."

"Except the subspace waves," he'd said.

Paris had smiled. The Captain had too. "Those aren't examples of hostiles, Mr. Neelix, although they are strange."

Neelix had shrugged and turned away, clearly unconvinced.

Paris hated the way the comments rolled in his head. He had to focus, instead of let old legends of abandoned places rise in his memory.

Paris aimed his tricorder at the nearest building and headed over to see if he could figure out how to get inside. What kind of buildings *were* these? Their walls were all windows, but none of the windows were open. People who wanted to see everything around them but didn't want to breathe it? Or maybe they only opened their windows at certain times of day or year.

The purple walkway led up to a curved section of the front of the building—or was it the back?—and stopped in a dead end. Paris saw nothing that resembled a door.

He cupped his hands above his eyes to cut the glare from the clear blue sky above and peered through the rosy, wire gridwork-impregnated glass. He could see what looked like a living room, though there wasn't furniture in it, only pits in the floor of varying depths and some shallower indentations that looked like good places to sit. Most of the floor was covered with something that looked fuzzy and comfortable. He couldn't tell what color it was through the colored glass.

"Hey, Tom." Torres, tricorder in hand and ex-

citement in her voice, was following Kes into the
park. "This way. Come on!"

Well, he was glad someone was excited about
something, Paris thought, waking out of an uneasy
trance. He didn't like what he was seeing in the
apartment. A round dish had fallen to the floor,
tipping its once-liquid contents across the carpet in
a messy streak. The stain appeared dry and caked-
on now, but it still looked sudden—eatus
interruptus—as if someone had vanished right out
from under his breakfast. And no one had come
along to clean up later.

Which struck him as odd, considering how
squeaky-clean this place was.

He turned and followed Torres, Kes, and Chakotay into the park, wondering what Torres was
worked up about.

She strode over to a statue of a humanoid
carrying a big leaf in an upright hand and stared at
it.

Paris liked the statue. If it was a war memorial,
he liked the way these people waged war. Fanned to
death by big leaves! Not quite what warrior Torres
would admire, though, so what was it about the
statue Torres was drawn to?

"The eyes of this statue are made of armacolite,"
she said, answering his unasked question. "Amazing." She fanned her tricorder around at the city.
"It's everywhere."

Paris didn't totally understand her excitement.
He hadn't been paying much attention to which

ship's materials were becoming scarce. He figured that wasn't his job. His job was to fly the ship. He'd let Captain Janeway and Torres do the worrying. They were much better at it.

Chakotay held his tricorder in front of him, then pointed. "The central energy source Ensign Kim located for us is this way," he said, gesturing across the park to another winding purple walkway.

"These people weren't big on mass transit," Paris said as the away team strolled over to the path. "What if they wanted to get somewhere in a hurry? Or, heaven forbid, wanted to carry something too large for one person with a wheelbarrow? Where are the cars? Where are the streets?"

"Maybe they had aircars," Chakotay said.

Paris glanced around. "If they did, the aircars were strange. There are no landing pads. The rooftops aren't even flat enough to land a VTOL vehicle on, and none of these weird buildings have docking bays. At least, I don't see any."

Chakotay grinned. "Maybe they levitated."

"Sure. Maybe that's what happened. They all got so happy one day they levitated right up to heaven," said Paris.

Chakotay shrugged. "Whatever they did, it didn't leave much of an energy trail. I don't even see any bicycles or other people-powered vehicles."

Torres pointed her tricorder downward and took some readings. "There are tunnels underground," she said.

"A subway?" Paris asked. "How quaint."

Torres's ridged brow furrowed farther. "Something's moving down there."

"Nothing alive," said Kes. "At least, nothing alive and intelligent in the way humanoids are." She held several silvery seeds on her palm. She paused long enough to slip them into a carry-pouch at her waist.

"How can you be sure without scanning?" Paris asked her. "I mean, I know Harry scanned the planet from orbit, but we always find things are a little different when we actually hit the pavement. How can you be so sure?"

"I'm . . ." Kes paused. "I'm just sure, that's all."

Paris didn't want to ask any more. Ever since Tuvok started helping Kes with her mental abilities, she had shown startling perceptiveness, the kind that made Paris nervous. It made him wonder what she knew about him that she wasn't telling.

"This is darned spooky," Paris said to cover his obvious discomfort with Kes's statement. He glanced around at the quiet buildings everywhere, the curving paths edged with greenery. These people hadn't even left footprints behind. "Where did everybody go? And why?"

"When we find out, you'll be the first to know," Torres said, exasperated. She tapped the controls on her tricorder. "The moving pieces underground are more machines."

"I'm getting that reading too," Chakotay said. "From their shapes, I'm guessing they're some sort of electric trains."

"They're running?" Paris asked.

"On schedule, but empty," Chakotay said.

"I don't get it," Torres said. "If these people were leaving, why didn't they turn out the lights?"

"Not everyone believes in conserving energy," Kes said.

"You have to admit this is strange," said Paris.

The other three just stared at him with lifted eyebrows. Torres wore half a smile.

"All right, don't admit it, then." Paris shrugged. Was he the only one disturbed by this empty city?

Watching the way Torres hunched her shoulders, he didn't think so. And Kes had already said it felt wrong. But he couldn't read Kes. She usually seemed calm, even when she wasn't.

They emerged into a different sort of neighborhood. The walkways were wider, the buildings bigger, and at their bases there were what looked like displays. Storefronts? Some of the windows were clear rather than colored glass here, and inside some of them were pasted sheets of pale-colored something with writing on it.

At one window Paris stopped to stare at a kinetic arrangement of slivers and slices of glass. At first he thought the many-colored glass pieces were floating on air, but further study showed him that each piece of jangling glass was supported on a nearly invisible thread. The glass pieces flickered and moved in waves, light glancing off their surfaces. The movement of light reminded him of a river he had flown over in a hovercraft at dawn.

"Tom, we don't have time for this," Torres said,

gripping his shoulder and shaking a little. "We need to find out as much as we can before the next pulse."

"Sorry," said Paris. "It's hypnotic."

"Seriously?" asked Chakotay.

Paris flickered his eyebrows up and down, wondering if this were a joke. No answering grin from Chakotay, so he said, "Naw, it's just some kind of art. I like it. I think."

They passed another storefront, and inside this one were holographic images of people wearing fancy clothes.

"Well, that answers one question," Paris said as he watched the moving display: A man and two women turned all the way around, then raised their arms and lowered them, to better display garments that draped and folded without binding tight anywhere. The man wore a narrow gold collar. One of the women was large, big-bellied and wide-hipped, and the other was slender. The large one's hair flowed in dark waves down around her shoulders and arms; the slender one had a hedge of reddish upstanding hair from her forehead down the back of her neck, like a mane, with her slightly pointed ears elegant against the bare sides of her skull. They both smiled. Paris liked the way both of them looked.

"Yes?" asked Chakotay.

"They're humanoid." It almost looked as though the slender one were waving at him.

"We could tell that from the statue," Torres said, exasperated again. "Besides, everything about this place is designed for humanoids." She gestured toward the pathway, the buildings, the storefronts.

Oh, yeah. The leaf-bearing statue with the armacolite eyes. "Oh. Pardon me for having "worn-out insights," Paris said. "I'll work on making them fresher next time."

"Tom," Kes said as she put her hand on his arm, "B'Elanna's just nervous."

"I heard that," Torres said. "And I'm not nervous. I'm impatient. I want to find out what's going on here, so we can leave with the armacolite."

"Sure, B'Elanna," Paris said. "Tell me again this empty place doesn't bother you. Tell me it doesn't make you think of Pompeii or the *Marie Celeste* or Ghitikana."

"All right," she said. "It doesn't remind me of Pompeii because the people are gone. It doesn't remind me of the *Marie Celeste* because I have no idea what that was. And it doesn't remind me of Ghitikana because those people didn't disappear, they beamed themselves to another planet. It just took the Federation two decades to find them."

"I wouldn't mess with her, Tom," Chakotay said softly.

"I heard that too," Torres said.

"For the record," Chakotay said, "this place makes me nervous as well."

The walkways widened into avenues, and then, suddenly, they reached the center of the city.

At least, it looked like the center. Sitting all by itself, surrounded by wide avenues, was a huge round building, covering more ground than any other building they'd seen so far. It was the first building with opaque white glass walls too.

And open doors. With ramps leading up to them, from all the sides that Paris could see.

"Definitely the central power nexus," Torres said, glancing from her tricorder to the building and back. "Let's get in there and look around."

They strode up one of the wide ramps.

Paris stopped on the threshold and stared. The center of the rotunda was empty space. A glass mosaic of many colors decorated a circle of floor five hundred meters across. The ceiling soared up into a vaulted dome through which daylight came, dazzling colored sparks out of the glass on the floor. Three hundred different room-sized, open-front booths formed a giant circle around the mosaic. Each booth could easily hold fifty to a hundred people. Above each booth was a sign with a word in this world's writing, inlaid with pieces of glass.

"What is this place?" Kes whispered, awe in her voice.

Torres moved forward, scanning as she went. Finally she said, "It's a transportation hub. These are all transporter booths."

"Here's your transportation system, Tom," Chakotay said.

"Well, that's one way to get around," Paris said.

Kes started toward one of the booths. Torres grabbed her arm. "I wouldn't do that."

"I was just going to take a closer look—"

"No," Torres said.

Paris understood before the other two did. "She's right," he said. "Stay away until we know what's going on. Those trains are still running. These things could be too."

CHAPTER
6

Time: The eighty-eighth shift
Location: 2,410 parallel universes to the right
of ours

THE WOMAN ON THE BIOBED WAS IN SO MUCH PAIN IT
hurt Kes to be near her. Kes grabbed her own
shoulder-length hair and pulled it into a ponytail to
get it out of the way. She hadn't had time to do that
since all of the casualties had come into sickbay.
She didn't have time now, but she needed her hair
to be back, out of the way, before she began
treating this woman.

This poor, poor woman. Her skin was a network
of burst capillaries, where it wasn't blotchy and
dark from its freezing exposure to the vacuum of
space. The whites of her eyes were solid red with
burst blood vessels and her face and clothes were
covered with freeze-dried blood that had bubbled
from her mouth and nose as her lungs collapsed.

Kes hyposprayed painkiller into the woman's
upper arm and glanced around sickbay. Everywhere she looked were more people, some in worse

states than this. The air was thick with the reek of death, near death, and disaster, so much damage and loss of control that the ship's filters couldn't keep up with it.

The autodoc extended its wings over the woman in the biobed and tried to heal the massive damage to all her organs. In addition to the soft-tissue effects of explosive decompression, the woman had several broken bones. Her life signs on the monitor were weak and erratic.

Kes was overwhelmed by the task before her. She tried to focus on each case, but that was difficult with so many needing treatment. She put up mental blocks, as Tuvok had taught her. It helped a little. She could shut out the wails of the dying in her head, but everywhere she looked she saw how much pain and devastation there was. There seemed no end to it.

All of the transporter rooms were running at capacity, beaming anyone with life signs from the ghost planet shape in the asteroid belt to *Voyager* as rapidly as possible.

Paris was out in the corridor with the rest of the dying, performing triage with the help of sixteen other crew members, deciding who might survive long enough to be helped in sickbay. Those Kes and the Doctor were working with were actually only a fraction of those beamed aboard.

Those too far gone were given painkillers and water, and helped or carried down to one of the empty cargo bays to await death in as much comfort as possible. Lieutenant Carey was converting one of the other cargo bays into an auxiliary sickbay.

Torres coaxed as much energy from her engines as she could; life support, medical use, and transporter overload were draining power almost faster than she could supply it.

Kes refilled her hypo and moved on to the next biobed, stepping over a groaning woman on the floor. The Doctor, a fierce frown on his face, was moving from biobed to biobed across the room, studying his medical tricorder and the life sign indicators. All too often he called one of the uniformed crew members to him and had people hauled back out into the corridor.

Sickbay door opened and Tuvok and Captain Janeway entered. Both of their faces were stoic as they picked their way past humanoid wreckage. The Doctor joined them in the center of sickbay, and Kes moved toward them, hypoing painkillers into people as she went.

"Will any of them make it?" Captain Janeway asked the Doctor in a low voice.

"I doubt it," the Doctor said. "They were exposed too long to open space."

The captain shook her head. A strand of hair slipped from the braid wrapped around the top of her head. She put her hand on the Doctor's arm. He looked startled at the contact. "Do what you can," she said.

"There isn't much I can do," he said. "We simply haven't the facilities to treat this kind of devastation. If you had warned me—"

"If I had been able to warn you," Captain Janeway said, "I might have been able to prevent this. It caught us by surprise."

"Captain," Tuvok said, "we do not have room for the additional wounded we're bringing aboard."

"I know, Tuvok." Captain Janeway sounded weary. "Convert part of the holodeck into an emergency center. Put some more crew members down there. I don't care if they have medical experience. Human contact has to count for something."

"It will ease some of the fear," Kes said.

She hoped. She hadn't really had time to see what kind of people these unfortunates were. All she knew was that they looked humanoid, and were in desperate need of help.

A woman reached up and grasped Kes's arm as she edged past a biobed. Kes looked at the readings near the bed. This woman wouldn't make it. She needed the Doctor to confirm, but she was certain. Already she knew what this sort of death looked like.

Then Captain Janeway was beside her. She glanced at Kes, her eyes asking the question. Would this woman survive? Kes shook her head no, and the Captain took a deep breath, then leaned over the woman.

"Can she speak?" Captain Janeway asked.

"Yes." The woman responded before Kes could. The woman's voice was a mere rasp, but it was clear, and she seemed eager to talk to someone.

"Can you tell me what happened?" Captain Janeway said with incredible compassion. Kes needed to move to another patient, but she couldn't. She needed to know the answer as badly as Captain Janeway did.

The woman gazed at Captain Janeway, then at the ceiling. "I was baking a cake," she said. "A celebration cake."

Then the woman closed her eyes and breathed her last.

CHAPTER 7

Time: The eighty-eighth shift
Location: 2,542 parallel universes to the right of ours

LIEUTENANT TORRES STOOD, HANDS IN FISTS ON HER hips, and stared around, halfway satisfied. She had a long rip in her red-and-green uniform, and grease of some sort on her arm, but she had the beginnings of an understanding.

It had taken them half an hour and many different types of tricorder scans to discover an access panel. The panel dropped down, using a piece of the mosaic floor to form a ramp to the main control room. The control room governed—so far as she could tell—the giant transportation system. Dim light shone, omnidirectional, from the pale gray ceiling. The underground air was fresh and just edging into cool, and carried almost no scent. Whatever these people used to filter their air, it worked.

Except for a faint whiff of newness—fresh paint, or just-dry glue. B'Elanna frowned. That was what she had been sensing above: the clear, bright mosaics, unscuffed by normal wear, and the roomy booths, without the slightest trace of soil or finger-printing. The grease on her arm had come from the access panel—and it was new, clean grease, the kind she used on *Voyager* when an automatic system wasn't working quite right and the problem was a flaw in the design. Below there wasn't a trace of dust. Either these people had the most efficient cleaning system ever developed, or this station was brand new.

Well, maybe both.

In the center of the room was a great pillar of clear glass, gridded at top and bottom with colored and lighted fibers and wires. Floating in the clear center of the pillar was a holographic translucent image of the planet, webbed with glowing route lines. Bright yellow nodes dotted the intersections of the routes. Many of the route lines drilled straight through the planet to touch surface on the opposite side.

Lighted control consoles formed a ring around the glass pillar, their tops low enough so that anyone seated at them could glance up and see the planet's image. The consoles rose from the floor like organic growths; at the work side of each of them there were footwells and furry seat cushions.

B'Elanna studied the map while the others explored.

Now that they had figured out how to work one door in the city, Paris was applying that information and discovering doors all over the place. He had already opened doors into corridors, closets, and restrooms, and now he was exploring an array of storage compartments, scanning contents and poking around for more.

Kes and Chakotay sat side by side on the floor in front of consoles, their feet in the footwells. They scanned the controls with their tricorders and murmured to each other about their discoveries.

B'Elanna walked all around the pillar, studying the holographic globe. Four of the route nodes were larger than the others, and colored white. One of the larger nodes corresponded to the away team's position on the east coast of the largest southern continent. She said, "This is one of the four main control stations for the entire planet."

She loved the elegant simplicity of it. The organization of function and style appealed to her. She felt that strange, satisfying déjà vu that always came over her when faced with something that made utter sense.

"How did they get whatever this is to work?" Paris muttered. He really wasn't examining anything in detail, and yet his findings were helpful. The layout of the control room was, in some indefinable way, essential to finding out how it all worked.

"Have you found the power source yet?" Chakotay asked. He lifted his feet out of the footwell and rose, aiming his tricorder in four cardinal directions and frowning at the readouts.

Torres dropped down in front of a control console, peering into the footwell before putting her feet in it. There was plenty of room. She kicked the walls, trying for a sense of space, and hit a control of some sort: The floor of the footwell rose until it was flat and supportive beneath her feet. She felt around the floor beside the seat cushion. Where would be the most logical place for another control? She put her hand there, and found another small bump. She pressed it. The floor rose up behind her into a comfortable and supportive chair back that conformed to her spine.

She smiled, liking the vanished race's design engineers. This congruence of thinking argued well for her being able to understand most of what she found here. She looked at the console, with its groupings of color-coded touch pads and graphic displays. Given time, she was sure she could be running this place.

"B'Elanna," Chakotay said in that soft, powerful way of his. He didn't have to say it twice.

"I'm not sure about the power source yet," she said, "but their access looks pretty direct. This place is exactly what I thought it was: a transporter station. I'm pretty sure it's configured differently from our transporters, but it gets the job done."

She stared at the consoles. In the upper right-hand corner of each one, a blue button was growing steadily brighter. "And I was right. The system is automated, and it's still working. In fact, I think it's gearing up for another run." She pulled her feet out of the footwell and jumped up, scanning for power transfer.

Now that she was looking for it, she got a sense of the power supply. Glancing up at the globe in the pillar, she confirmed her suspicions. Below the route lines was another network, almost like nerves or a bloodstream, with branches all through the planet's crust. This buried network was glowing brighter, like the console buttons. "It's charging," she said, more to herself than to Chakotay. "It uses power from every conceivable source. Solar, geothermal, wind. They've thought of everything."

"That's a tremendous amount of power," Chakotay said. He stopped behind her and looked over her shoulder. "What were they trying to do?"

"The first question is how did they store it?" she said, speaking rapidly, as she always did when she was learning. She ran her tricorder over the console. "All the power sources drain into a huge power reservoir under the station—well, under these four stations, though there are lesser reservoirs elsewhere."

She touched a button on the console and the four major nodes brightened. "When the reservoir reaches maximum charge, it transports."

She stared at the globe, the filaments of route lines leading from one node to the next. "It transports anybody in those booths. Each booth has a specific destination."

The route lines were falling into place in her mental map.

"The ultimate commute," said Paris, coming to stand beside her and Chakotay. He sounded more interested than surprised. People had been using transporter technology to commute on Earth for years, and other races humans had met had independently developed their own forms of transportation. It was one of those instances of parallel evolution of technology: Every spacefaring race eventually discovered some form of transporter, as they did warp drive. The only real difference was in the development. B'Elanna had never seen this sort of power configuration before.

She tapped her teeth with her index finger. "This charges every two and a half hours. Whoever's in a booth goes to whatever destination they've chosen. Every two and a half hours."

"Like the subspace pulses," said Kes.

"Yes," said B'Elanna. "That's right. The subspace pulses are a byproduct of this worldwide transport system."

"Do you think this system," Kes asked, staring up at the holographic globe, "has something to do with all the people disappearing?"

"I don't know," said B'Elanna. "Not yet." She itched to get her hands on a console here. "Let's see what we can find out."

CHAPTER
8

Time: The eighty-eighth shift
Location: Our universe

JANEWAY SAT IN HER COMMAND CHAIR, HER CONSOLE still up. She was monitoring the data from the planet, analyzing, as best she could, some of the information from the subspace waves. Tuvok and Harry Kim were evaluating the data in more depth, but she kept an eye on the proceedings. Lieutenant Torres had the best technical mind on *Voyager,* but Torres was on the surface, where she was needed. Janeway's scientific knowledge came second, and sometimes she wished she had more time to sift data herself.

Those other ships, other *Voyagers,* bothered her. A reflection didn't usually have a gap in it. And seeing all those *Voyagers* put her in mind of the time she had nearly sacrificed her own ship to save another *Voyager.* The fact that she hadn't—that the other *Voyager* sacrificed itself to save her ship—haunted her nights.

It was also haunting her right now, for a reason

she couldn't pinpoint. The obvious answer was that seeing the other *Voyager*s triggered the memory, but Janeway had learned to be leery of the obvious answer.

Neelix had come to the bridge shortly after Kes left. He didn't like to be away from her. Kes tolerated a lot more contact than Janeway would: Neelix checking on her when she worked in sickbay; Neelix hovering over her when she ate; Neelix guarding her every move. But he seemed particularly vulnerable when he was on the ship and she wasn't. He had developed the habit of coming to the bridge in that circumstance, and Janeway hadn't discouraged it. Many times, Neelix had provided just the right information at just the right time.

She was getting nowhere on her work. Her mind was too busy with the details of command, with worrying about the bridge crew, the away team, the timing of the next subspace pulse. She found herself wondering what she would see during that pulse. More *Voyager*s? Or something else entirely?

"How is the data analysis coming along, Mr. Tuvok?" Janeway asked.

"It is proceeding, Captain." There was a frown in the Vulcan's voice.

Near the turbolift Neelix raised a hand to his face. "I'm worried, Captain. Kes is down there, and things are not right."

"I know, Neelix," Janeway said. "We're taking every precaution with the away team."

Every precaution they could take, in any event.

There was some risk. There was always some risk. That was part of the business.

"Thank you, Captain," Neelix said, in that curiously humble way he had when he felt someone had done him a kindness. "I know you'll watch out for my Kes."

"Captain," Kim said, "I'm getting the away team's tricorder scans."

"Wonderful, Ensign," Janeway said. "Please add them to the data pool and tell me if you find anything."

She could hear the bleeps and blips as he worked the console. "So far," he said, "the picture is not getting any clearer."

"How long until the next subspace event, Mr. Tuvok?" Janeway asked.

"Captain," Kim said, before Tuvok could respond. "I'm reading a large energy buildup below the away team."

"I concur with Mr. Kim's conclusion, Captain," said Tuvok. "Power is massing at hundreds of locations on Birsiba. I believe this is preparatory to another of the subspace discharges."

"Ensign Kim, open a channel to the away team."

"Aye, Captain," Kim said. "The channel is open."

"Commander Chakotay," Janeway said. "We are reading a large energy buildup near you. Can you confirm this?"

Chakotay's voice came back broken and garbled. Then it was cut off.

She didn't like that at all. "Get him back on-line," she said.

Neelix had moved closer to the command chairs. He clutched the railing behind Chakotay's chair.

"Captain," Kim said, "the energy buildup is interfering with our communications." He worked over his console. "I'm reconfiguring our sensors to see if I can get clearer reception." He frowned down at his equipment after working with it fruitlessly for a moment or so. Then he looked up at Janeway and shook his head.

"Let's get them out of there," she said.

"With that much energy buildup right below them, Captain," Tuvok said, "we dare not attempt a transport until they move a safe distance away. We would risk losing them."

"Losing them!" Neelix said.

Janeway ignored him. "Ensign, contact R'Lee. We talked to him just before the last discharge. They must have a communications system that compensates for the high energy buildup. Get him and then figure out how they do it."

A moment later R'Lee came on the screen. He was still wearing the blue toga-like outfit and the silver necklace. He did not look surprised to see her, which relieved her more than she wanted to admit.

"Captain," he said. "It is such a pleasure to hear from you."

"This is not a social call, R'Lee."

He bobbed. "Of course not. You have called about your 'away team.' Such a quaint name for such a long distance traveled! They are, as they have told me, making headway."

"I'd like to talk to one of them," Janeway said.

"Surely a ship as wondrous as yours has its own communication system," R'Lee said.

"Yes," Janeway said, "it does. But the energy buildup on your planet seems to be blocking our normal channels of communication. I need your help reaching our team."

"It is of no problem. I will direct your communication to them through one of our systems. The line shall be open, and, of course, private."

"Thank you, R'Lee," Janeway said. She liked his reassurance that the line would be private, although she knew better than to trust that from anyone.

R'Lee's face disappeared, the screen went momentarily blank, and then Chakotay's face greeted her. He looked preoccupied. Behind him, Torres sat at a control panel, scanning it with her tricorder.

"Captain, you did receive my last message?" Chakotay asked.

"You were cut off." She had no time for chitchat. "We're reading a large energy buildup near you. Because of it, we're having trouble reaching you through our own communication system. I tried to beam you aboard, but the energy buildup interfered."

"I don't think it's necessary to leave just yet, Captain," Chakotay said. "We're reading the buildup too. Lieutenant Torres says it is their transport system gearing up. She wants to study it more."

"Fine," Janeway said. "But at the first sign of trouble, I want you out of there. We cannot beam you aboard when you are near that energy source, so move away from it as quickly as you can. We will have a lock on you, and we will beam you up immediately."

"Captain, I don't think there'll be any trouble," Chakotay said. "It's a new system and the people here just aren't used to it."

"Still, Chakotay," Janeway said, "I don't like being out of touch with my away team."

Chakotay smiled. "I understand, Captain."

"Now," she said, "you were trying to contact me?"

He nodded. "I was letting you know about that medical matter we discussed," he said. He had to be referring to R'Lee.

"R'Lee assures me this line is private," Janeway said, "but sensitive information should wait until you return to the ship."

"I understand," Chakotay said. "But I can tell you this: Kes did a medical scan of the subject and found nothing obviously unusual. We cannot account for culture or differences in biology, but I do believe the anomalies he mentioned, and the ones we saw, do exist. And I believe they are external."

"Caused by the pulse?"

"I cannot say, Captain. We need a bit more time."

"You may not have it, Chakotay. We believe that energy buildup below you—"

"That it is the beginning of the pulse," Chakotay finished. "I know. Torres has already noticed the same thing."

"There is a risk, Chakotay, that this pulse could have a physical effect on you."

He nodded. "It is a risk we're all willing to take."

"I don't like it," Neelix said from behind her.

"Mr. Neelix," Janeway said.

He pursed his lips, but said no more.

"Take whatever precautions you can," Janeway said, "and uplink the information you gather as quickly as possible."

"Aye, Captain," Chakotay said.

"And Chakotay, if there is another effect like the mirror effect we saw earlier, let me know. It may be on a smaller scale on the planet itself, presenting as a trick of the light or a slight shaking of images. Whatever you see, no matter how small, whatever changes you detect, no matter how insignificant, report to us."

"Aye, Captain," he said. He smiled at her. "We will be back in touch after the surge is over. Chakotay out."

His image disappeared before she could sign off. He understood. She knew he understood. But she wanted to explain it to him again in the clearest language she knew:

If something happens down there, Chakotay, we can do nothing. You're on your own until the pulse ends. No matter what the danger, you're on your own.

"I don't like this, Captain," Neelix said.

"They'll be all right, Mr. Neelix," she said—and hoped she wasn't making any false promises.

CHAPTER 9

Time: The eighty-eighth shift
Location: 2,542 parallel universes to the right
of ours

CHAKOTAY RUBBED THE TATTOO ON HIS CHEEK. HE
touched it on occasion when something moved
him or perplexed him. It was a habit he had gotten
into at the Academy, when he needed a reminder
of who he was and where he came from.

He needed to remember that now, as he stood in
the transporter control center on an abandoned
planet.

The planet's emptiness disturbed him partly
because he found so much to admire about the
place itself. He liked the way the vanished people
had incorporated green life into their cityscape.
Though the plants in the many small parks the
away team had passed on their journey to the
transport hub had been ordered and groomed in a
way that rendered them tame, still, there were a lot
of them, and they seemed strong, well watered, and
contented. They gave the city's air a constant

70

undertone of greenery and flowers and running water.

The huge transport building had its own charms. The mosaics on the main floor created abstract patterns that almost made sense to him. He had tried looking at them out the corners of his eyes; sometimes he could see better with a sideways glance than a direct stare. In his peripheral vision, the swirls of colored chips had shifted into something resembling writing. He would have liked to study the mosaics further, but there was no time for nonessentials.

In the control room below he studied the situation-responsive elements in the planetary image in the center of the room. Torres's interpretation of the power-grid ramping up for another pulse made perfect sense. The filaments and capillaries of power sources lacing the crust of the hologlobe glowed brighter and brighter.

There was a danger in choosing the simplest interpretation of any situation, Occam's razor notwithstanding. Just because Torres's hypotheses made sense, that didn't make them correct.

She did have a more immediate grasp of systems than he did, though. In his experience, she was almost always right about engineering matters. He tapped his commbadge. *"Voyager,"* he said. *"Voyager,* come in."

His badge chirped, then emitted static. He tapped it again, but the static didn't clear.

Torres scanned the area around them, then snapped her tricorder closed. "The power buildup below and around us is blocking communication with *Voyager.*"

"And transporter capability?" Chakotay asked.

"It's blocking that too," Torres said. "We'll need to move a safe distance away from the station if we want to communicate or transport. Right now we're in the corona of a gathering power matrix."

"Is that dangerous to our health?" Kes wondered.

"I don't know," Torres said. "We still don't know what caused these people to vanish."

"I sure hope it's not this," Paris said.

"As do we all," Chakotay said. "Torres?"

"Usually," she said, "the kind of energy that wipes out living beings destroys plants as well."

"Then we go back to my original question," Kes said. "Will this power surge harm us?"

"I doubt it," Torres said. "It would be silly to design a station like this for people to use if it could harm them."

"All species are different," Kes said. "We've never seen the people who created these systems. We don't know how they were composed. Our systems are largely electrical. At some level, high concentrations of energy could disrupt neural firing and synaptic responses."

"Let alone our brains," said Paris.

"This energy isn't precisely electrical," Torres said. "Somewhere along the way between its sources and the giant power matrix here, it's modulated into something I don't quite recognize."

Chakotay frowned at her. "What do you mean?"

She ran the tricorder over the console. "Give me a moment, Chakotay," she said. "It would take too long to explain."

"How much time until the next subspace discharge?" Paris asked.

"Fifty-five minutes," Torres said.

"Could we survive a discharge here on the planet?" Kes asked.

Torres glanced at Chakotay and shrugged. "I don't see why not. The subspace energy that accompanies the pulse isn't strong enough to hurt us."

"Maybe that's what the people who lived here thought right before they disappeared," Paris said.

Chakotay recognized the look on Torres's face. She wanted to stay, to learn exactly what was happening with the energy pulse.

"You can monitor it from above the planet," Chakotay said.

"It won't be the same," Torres responded, confirming his suspicion. She would stay here at any cost. "We'll be fine."

Chakotay shook his head. "I don't trust it. We're going to monitor the next energy surge from orbit. Then we'll come back and see what's changed."

"It is the more prudent course, Torres," Paris said.

"Imagine you lecturing me on prudent courses," she said.

"Look," Paris said, "these people vanished in the middle of whatever they were doing. I kinda like my life. I don't want to vanish suddenly. Who knows where I'll end up?"

"Well, we're not going to find out," Chakotay said. "Let's get out of this corona into range of *Voyager*'s transporters."

Paris and Kes headed for the ramp. Torres didn't move. "Chakotay, this could be a type of energy we can tap—"

"No arguments, Torres," he said. "We've got some hiking to do."

CHAPTER
10

Time: The eighty-eighth shift
Location: 2,542 parallel universes to the right
of ours

CAPTAIN KATHRYN JANEWAY RAN A HAND THROUGH
her short hair. She still was uncomfortable with its
length, and with the absence of weight. She had let
Ensign Starr talk her into a haircut only a few
hours before this crisis started.

The away team was raising more questions than
they were resolving.

"We cannot break through the energy buildup,"
Tuvok said. "It is interfering with transporters as
well as communication."

Janeway already knew that would happen. If the
ship couldn't contact the away team, it couldn't
lock onto the commbadges either. It was only in
rare instances when the transporters worked and
communication didn't.

"Mr. Kim," Janeway said. "Is there any way to
block that interference long enough to beam the
away team back aboard?"

Kim looked worried. "I don't think so, Captain."

She needed Lieutenant Torres. But Torres was on the planet.

"Is that buildup going to harm my away team?"

"I don't think so," Kim said, "but it's strong enough and complex enough to scramble any communication."

"Well, nothing blocks communication forever," Janeway said. "We just haven't found the solution yet. Keep at it, Mr. Kim."

"Aye, sir," he said.

Perhaps they needed to change how they were looking at the energy buildup, to find another solution.

"Do we know the cause of that buildup?" she asked Tuvok.

"It is planetwide," he said. "And seems to be originating near the away team itself."

"Are we causing it?"

"No, Captain," Kim said. "This is the source of the subspace pulse."

"I don't like it," Janeway said. "This planet is recently abandoned, and it has an unusual energy buildup that is the source of unusual subspace waves. Despite your reassurances, Mr. Kim, I refuse to see this buildup as benign. We need to get the away team off the planet, and we need to do so quickly."

"Captain," Tuvok said, "we would be able to get a shuttlecraft to the away team before the energy reaches its peak. However, we could not get the shuttlecraft off the planet before the next subspace wave."

"Mr. Kim," Janeway said, "Have those waves had any effect on *Voyager?*"

"Only small ones, Captain," he said. "We could feel the waves, but it didn't hurt the ship in any way."

"Send the shuttlecraft, Mr. Tuvok. They can get inside and be shielded from the energy's effects, perhaps better than on the planet itself."

"It does seem the logical solution," Tuvok said.

"Captain!" Kim said. "The away team is moving."

"Moving?" Janeway asked. "Where?"

Kim studied his instruments for a moment, then looked up. "Toward the edge of the city. It seems they are trying to get away from the energy source."

"Will that be distance enough to reestablish communication?"

"I believe so," Kim said.

"Tuvok," Janeway said, "belay my previous order. I would rather beam them out of there than send a shuttlecraft and another person into that energy field."

"Aye, Captain," Tuvok said.

"Mr. Kim," Janeway said, "will they make it to the city's edge before the next wave hits?"

"I think so," he said.

She took a deep breath. It was a risk she would have to take. "Keep trying to figure out a way to block that interference, Mr. Kim. The second you do, beam them aboard."

"Yes, Captain," Kim said.

Janeway sat down in her Captain's chair and stared at the viewscreen. She had expected the away team to be done by now, not to have discovered more questions. The more she learned, the less she liked. People interrupted midmeal, a normally neat place with one untidy spot, transportation equipment running, an unexplained energy buildup.

The subspace waves seemed to be the symptom of a problem, a problem she suspected was much greater than she had initially realized.

Obviously someone on the away team—probably Chakotay—had realized it too. He was getting them to move to transporter range.

She hoped it would work.

CHAPTER
11

Time: The eighty-eighth shift
Location: 2,410 parallel universes to the right
of ours

THE SMELL OF DEATH AND DISASTER PERMEATED THE
conference room. Janeway studied her senior officers, who sat slumped around the polished black
table in attitudes of weary defeat. They had just
spent an hour and a half trying to help hundreds of
doomed people, and they hadn't succeeded in
saving a single life. Worse, they had seen in space
the death agonies of billions they didn't even have
the ability to save.

The task before them had been enormous. *Voyager* couldn't house billions of humanoids, even if
the humanoids had been healthy. To attempt to
save several hundred had felt like trying to empty
an ocean with a bucket. And those hundred had
been too far gone, the damage to their organs too
far along, to save.

No one looked out the viewports, where the gray
and tortured edge of the graveyard planet was

visible. Everyone had seen a fraction of what was out there, right up close.

Janeway could feel the exhaustion in her own limbs. She could see it on the faces of the others.

Neelix sat with his arm around Kes's shoulder. Kes's blood-spattered gray tunic and the dark circles under her eyes bore testament to her unceasing efforts in sickbay. Neelix's crest was matted with dried blood, and his facial spots stood out against his unnaturally pale skin. He had gone among the dying, doing his best to offer comfort. Janeway wondered if he felt he had succeeded. It would be nice if any of them could have felt that. His chartreuse eyes looked glazed and sad.

Chakotay's cheekbones seemed more pronounced, the mandala tattoo on his left cheek darker. He sat with his hand on the table in front of him, his fingers curled around a pale stone. He seemed to be drawing comfort, or at least calm, from the stone. His shoulders were relaxing, increment by increment.

Paris leaned back in his chair, his head pushed back against the headrest and his eyes closed. He too looked pale, exhausted, and brushed everywhere with dried brown blood.

Beside him, Kim sat with hunched shoulders, staring down at his hands. He had spent the crisis helping Torres in engineering as she worked to reroute power into the systems they needed most.

Even Tuvok's dark face looked ashen.

Torres's hands were fisted before her, and her

brows were lowered over her fierce eyes. She looked ready for a fight.

But how could they fight this? Janeway wondered, not for the first time. She had never felt so discouraged. She had watched an incomprehensible number of people die a horrible, painful, senseless death.

She had known that the same thing had happened repeatedly before the ship had arrived.

And worse yet, she suspected that it would happen again and again in the future, if they didn't find a way to stop it.

In some small silent part of her, she wished they had never come here. She could give the order to leave, but that didn't feel right. How could she turn her back on billions dying? It wasn't possible.

Of those around the table, only the Doctor, able to be present in the conference room because of his mobile holoemitter, looked unaffected by what they had just gone through. Janeway knew it had affected him, however.

She had seen him in one of the corridors, attempting to revive a young girl. "Come on," he had been whispering over and over. "I can get you through this. You must survive. You must!"

"There were no survivors," the Doctor said in his matter-of-fact way, as if any of them needed to be told. "What would you like me to do with the bodies?"

How could they honor this infinity of the dead? Janeway pressed the heel of her palm to her forehead for a moment, trying to ease the weight of despair that bowed her shoulders and bent her neck forward. None of the dying had lived long enough to give anyone an idea of their burial customs.

Janeway glanced around at her officers, considered her options, then made the sensible choice. "Have them beamed back into space," she said, and sighed.

The room was deathly silent. Only Tuvok met her eyes. He offered her a morsel of comfort, a brief nod at the logic of the decision.

Janeway straightened, drew in a deep breath, let it out. Time to rise out of this dark place and consider their next steps. The crew was demoralized, and so was she. The only way to turn this around was to turn herself around. And the only way to do that was to take charge of the situation as best she could.

"All right," she said. "We couldn't save this group of people. We did what we could, and it wasn't enough. I'm not satisfied with what happened, but we can't let this defeat us. There were bodies before we got here, and another group arrived while we were here. Therefore, it's reasonable to assume that more will arrive in the next subspace event. We need to have a plan in place. A twofold plan. First off, the next time living beings get beamed into space, I want to be able to save them."

Her strong voice had caught the attention of the crew. Paris sat forward and opened his eyes. Neelix kept his arm around Kes, but she sat up, as if Janeway had snapped her to attention.

"Second, and most important, I want to figure out what causes this and stop it. Period."

Around the table she had all their attention.

"First, let's discuss what we know, and then let's move into what we can do."

Tuvok took the lead first, as she knew he would.

"The bodies started appearing," Tuvok said, "exactly two-hundred-twenty-one-point-five hours ago, at the same time as the subspace disturbances began radiating from this system."

Janeway nodded. "The bodies and the subspace disturbances are connected. We don't yet know how. What else do we know?"

Ensign Kim cleared his throat. "The multiple asteroid belts and planets we saw during the event seem to be echoes from parallel universes. The same goes for the other *Voyager*s we saw."

"But why *Voyager*s only every other universe?" Neelix asked.

"I've been thinking about that," Janeway said. "Remember when we encountered the other *Voyager* in that plasma cloud when we were trying to escape the Vidiians?"

Neelix nodded, still confused.

Janeway stared down at her hands, which clasped each other on the table before her. It was still difficult to think about that encounter with herself. She had stood face to face with herself, saw much to admire, and some things that still troubled her. What she couldn't question was her stubbornness and integrity; her other self, knowing that one of the two *Voyager*s was doomed, had made the decision to self-destruct her own ship and everyone on it.

Janeway had made that decision first, and would have done it had her counterpart not asked her to wait fifteen minutes. In that stretch of time, the other Janeway's ship was invaded by Vidiians, and her crew, outnumbered and outgunned, had already largely fallen before the organ harvesters. The self-destruction of the other *Voyager* had destroyed the Vidiian ship as well, before it could locate and pillage this *Voyager*.

Her counterpart's sacrifice had saved Janeway's own *Voyager* in more ways than one, and she sometimes woke in the night with a huge ache in her heart and the taste of metal on her tongue.

If only . . .

If only . . .

If only they had had enough time to come up with a different solution.

If only the Vidiians hadn't found them again.

If only she had been the one to self-destruct, she would not have to lie awake some nights dream-deep in unbearable regrets.

Janeway glanced at Ensign Harry Kim, who had come to this *Voyager* across a spatial rift from that separate, but very similar reality. Did he still lie awake wondering about that event? His dark eyes met hers, and she got the impression that it did still trouble him. In a way, everyone he knew and had worked with up until that moment had died—even though he still saw the same people every day.

"When that happened," Janeway said, moving her thoughts back to the conversation at hand, "we believed that the plasma storm had taken *Voyager* out of phase with itself, and created the other *Voyager*. I had assumed that the situation was similar to the one created in a controlled experiment at Starfleet Academy, and that the results would be the same."

"Are you saying you were wrong, Captain?" Paris asked.

"I don't think so, Tom," Janeway said, "but I do think my assumptions were incomplete. I believe we witnessed an even more fundamental change, and didn't—or couldn't—see all that occurred."

"What do you mean?" Neelix asked.

She said, "I suspect that event was a primary branch on a decision tree, and split off two parallel universes, one with *Voyager,* one without."

Suddenly Neelix's face lit up with understanding. "So in all the parallel universes that exist, every other *Voyager* was destroyed because it met up with the one in the universe beside it?"

"That would be my guess," Janeway said.

"But," Tuvok said, "if that were the case, then the second ship we encountered, the *Voyager* that was destroyed, destroyed itself because of Vidiians. Both ships were menaced by the same Vidiian ship. If we were in parallel universes, there would have been another Vidiian ship."

"Not necessarily," Janeway said. "Because that

was the point from which the parallel universe split off, leaving one with a *Voyager,* one without."

"So there are an infinite number of *Voyager*s," Ensign Kim said.

"An infinite number of universes," Janeway said. "Some with *Voyager,* and some without."

"But," Chakotay said, "in most of those other universes, the planet that used to be here is still intact."

Kim nodded. "From our computer analysis of the images, that's the case for at least two thousand universes in both directions, except for the hundred and thirty to our left. That's as much as we can determine from our recordings."

"Why would that happen?" Paris said. "If our universes are parallel, shouldn't the events that occur be parallel as well?"

"Not necessarily, Tom," Janeway said.

Torres shook her head in hard agreement with Janeway. "Details would change. It's like a copy of a copy of a copy. Eventually even fundamental things would be different. Enough that in a few universes a planet would be destroyed by an event while in other universes it wouldn't."

Janeway glanced around at her crew. The energy of looking for a solution was slowly pushing back the events of the last hour. It was a start.

"But this is the only universe with . . ." Neelix glanced quickly over his shoulder at the mass of dead bodies out the viewport.

Janeway drew in a breath and let it out slowly. "Which leads to speculations," she said. "Apparently, whatever this subspace phenomenon is, it shifts people from one universe to another in only one direction. Those who come here to die . . ." She frowned a moment, then straightened her shoulders. "They come from the intact planet in the universe to our right."

She let those words sink in. In that world now, there were another three and a half billion humanoids going about their lives without any understanding that in a very short time they will suddenly find themselves floating in the cold of space.

"Ensign Kim, have you been able to study the final asteroid-belt universe to our left before the next intact planet?"

"I've run as many analyses on the images as I can, Captain," Kim said.

"There is no graveyard there, is there?"

"No."

"Which supports your hypothesis, Captain," Tuvok said. "And implies a further one."

"Go on, Lieutenant."

"The event transports only living humanoids. This is the first asteroid-belt universe to the left of an intact planet, and the humanoids make that transition, but they do not move into the next universe with the subsequent event. The main change in their status is that they have died in the interim."

Janeway nodded. "My conclusion as well."

"But that means that—" Paris said. He paled and visibly swallowed.

"Yes," said Janeway, shaking her head slowly in agreement.

"Means what?" Neelix asked.

"It's going to happen again. And again." Paris licked his upper lip. "Every two and a half hours, Captain? Another planet full of people will die?"

She wished there were another answer she could give him.

Torres hit the table with her fist. "We've got to do something!"

"I am open to suggestions," said Janeway.

"We could prepare for it better now that we know what to expect," Chakotay said. "Move in closer, catch the people sooner. If their anatomy is similar to ours they ought to be able to survive a few moments of vacuum and recover."

"But how do we pick who to save?" asked Paris. "We can't get a whole planet full of people on *Voyager* every two and a half hours. We don't have the space, we don't have the facilities, and we don't have the energy."

"What if we don't have to get them aboard?" Torres said.

"What do you have in mind, Lieutenant?" asked Janeway. She could see Torres's excitement building.

"Containment fields. Suppose we could project a big bubble full of atmosphere out there? Maybe it would keep people alive long enough for us to come up with some sort of rescue idea—"

"The sixth planet in the system could be terraformed," Kim broke in, catching excitement from

Torres. "It already has early-stage atmosphere, and—"

"Terraforming is the work of years," said Tuvok, "and even terraformed, that planet could not possibly support an endless stream of the billions that will be coming here if this subspace event continues indefinitely."

"Oh," Kim said, defeated by her understanding of what Tuvok was saying.

"It could buy us some time, though," said Janeway. "We could at least do a rough-and-ready settlement plan, blast out a cavern and seal it for atmosphere—"

"The logistics of providing food and water for so many people, or even a breathable atmosphere, are staggering, and beyond our capabilities, Captain," said Tuvok.

"You are probably right, Tuvok," Janeway said, feeling exhaustion in every fiber of her being. "But it's better to try something, anything, than sit idly by."

"I do not agree, Captain," Tuvok said in a low tone. "Logically, our own survival is our first priority; exhausting our resources in a futile attempt to solve an insurmountable problem is counterproductive."

Logically, Janeway wondered if her security officer was right. But the thought of doing nothing overwhelmed any logic.

At this point, all she knew was that eighty-eight entire planetary populations had already been lost. This had to be stopped.

Somehow.

"We save who we can," she said. "But most importantly, we work on a way to stop this. Understand?"

Everyone nodded.

She just wished she believed it were possible.

CHAPTER
12

Time: The eighty-eighth shift
Location: Our universe

THE CONTROL ROOM OF ONE OF BIRSIBA'S FOUR MAIN transportation hubs was full of people. The underground room was huge, and so was the crowd. Chakotay was surprised at how pleasant so many people packed so tight could smell. Nice body odor must be a species trait; he knew that when he worked long hours in close quarters with humans and human–other species mixes, he never felt this way. He didn't even like his own smell after a long sweaty day.

Birsibans smelled nice, and they were incredibly pleasant to deal with, if a bit vague. R'Lee, the head of the World Council, was actually not the only head of the World Council. He shared the title with Lelah Bir and Fando Jee. There were at least three people of every rank, so there was no such thing as a swift or independent decision.

Chakotay wasn't sure exactly how the system worked, but he suspected, after watching the Birsibans interact, that there was a small bit of telepathy involved. Not enough to make things easier for him, but enough to make oblique the communication between the three people of a particular rank.

He hated it.

It had taken the away team more than half an hour to determine that no one in the control room was actually a scientist who could explain to them how the transporter technology was supposed to work, or what they had discovered, if anything, about why it was malfunctioning—everyone here was either a planetary administrator, a transportation coordinator, or a news hound.

Torres had ignored various diplomatic protocols and gotten to work scanning with her tricorder, edging some of the workers aside so she could study their consoles, asking questions about computer operations, their method of embedding their computers in smartglass, and the holographic globe in the room's center.

Paris was still trying to get someone to tell him where the "round-the-clock" science teams were. He had consulted with a number of women, but didn't seem to have gotten any information.

Kes, at least, had focused on Lelah Bir and Fando Jee in her quest for knowledge. Chakotay had never seen the small, slender Ocampan exhibit anger or frustration—she was always warm and helpful—but right at this moment her face looked frustrated. He would have been amused if he hadn't felt so frustrated himself.

"Look," Chakotay said to R'Lee at last, "you've

asked us for help, but you're hindering our ability to give it to you. How can we work together on this? We need to talk to people who can give us real answers, and we need that *now*. The next subspace pulse is due in ten minutes."

"Let me consult with my others," R'Lee said, heading toward Bir and Jee, who, accompanied by Kes, were making their way toward R'Lee. What a time for them to finally get together, thought Chakotay. He followed, exasperated, wondering if there was any way to make these reasonable-appearing people see reason.

"The science teams are in some other building," Kes said before the world councilors could greet each other formally again, "in another city."

Chakotay breathed out anger and breathed in calm. "We're going to have to wait out this pulse before we can get some answers, then," he said, wondering how long it would take to get R'Lee or someone else to set up communications so they could conference long-distance with the science teams. What were the odds of getting straight answers from Birsiban scientists? he wondered. These people were obsessed with triplicates, which made their thinking more convoluted and less accessible than people who polarized everything. Maybe that explained why their engineering was as baffling as it was.

He wondered if Torres was having any luck in her explorations. He spotted her. She was shaking a fist in someone's face.

"Lieutenant!" he called.

She turned to look at him over the heads of the crowd. Her eyes were wide, dark, and furious.

He gestured for her to join him, and she plowed right past those around her, leaving shocked faces in her wake.

"Honestly," she said, "I ask you, what use are reporters? All they do is interrupt and ask stupid questions! I want some answers myself—about something real!"

"I'm very sorry," said R'Lee. "Our contact with other spacefaring races has been minimal. We forget that not everyone has the same priorities we do."

"Why isn't your priority this strange event that changes everything every two and a half hours?" Torres demanded. "We should be working on getting it stopped!"

"That *is* my priority," he said.

"But not mine," said Jee.

"Or mine," said Bir.

Torres growled. Her hands curled into claws.

"Lieutenant Torres," Chakotay said, his voice dangerously calm.

She turned and glared at him. He gave her his best stern gaze in return, and after a moment, her shoulders dropped and her fingers relaxed.

"Check the time," he said.

She glanced at her tricorder. "One minute until the next event. One minute? One minute, and we know almost less now than we did before we got here!"

"What do we know?"

She snorted, then calmed. "We're standing on a huge power matrix that has been gathering energy for the past two and a half hours. There are four of these major matrices spaced equidistant around the planet, and a number of smaller ones. The idea was that these matrices collect power from a multitude of sources and store it until repletion arrives, and every time the reservoirs are replete, they activate transportation of anyone in the booths above, sending them to whichever destination a specific booth is linked to. Only this doesn't seem to work at all. People in the booths don't exactly get transported. Instead, every two and a half hours, a light comes out of the sky, and——"

She glanced at her tricorder. "Time," she said.

Chakotay held his tricorder in front of him as the room filled with white light. The light was so intense it washed away all details until he was standing in a core of relentless omnidirectional light. He sensed himself moving slightly, as if floating.

Then the light vanished, and the room, with its central column containing a large globe, and its teeming people, was still intact. Weight settled on his body.

And everything looked normal.

"This isn't right," Torres said, staring at her tricorder. Her fingers moved over the controls and she watched the readout, then made it repeat.

"What is it?" Chakotay said.

"The power," she said. "Check these readings."

Chakotay watched data stream across her tricorder's readout. The readings made no sense. The power in that last surge was thousands and thousands of times greater than the planet's total reserves. That wasn't possible. Where had all the extra power come from?

Chakotay looked at Torres.

"What the hell is going on here?" she said. "I'm going to get some answers out of these people if I have to knock heads to do it!" She glared at R'Lee.

He frowned at her.

She made a snort of disgust and headed away from him into the crowd, apparently to see if she could find some answers from someone else.

Paris emerged from the crowd, trailed by two women. "Sir," he said, his voice urgent. "I think we have a problem."

Chakotay turned to Paris. His face was white as he stared at his tricorder. Then he looked up at Chakotay. *"Voyager*'s gone."

CHAPTER 13

Time: The eighty-eighth shift
Location: 2,542 parallel universes to the right
of ours

JANEWAY SAT IN HER CAPTAIN'S CHAIR AND STUDIED
visuals from the tricorder readings the away team
had sent from the empty planet below, before the
energy buildup interfered with communication. As
she did so, she had the computer scan the readings
for any anomalies, anything to suggest what had
happened to the population. Her bridge crew was
searching for the same information by scanning the
planet, but she felt this microscopic approach
might be successful. Between her own analysis and
the computer's, she might find something.

Anything.

In front of her the main screen showed a clear
image of the beautiful planet, but at the moment
she was more interested in the report her Chief
Engineer had transmitted back playing out on her
chair screen.

Torres had sent the image of a white glass statue
with armacolite eyes, an interesting use of a non-

gloss malleable metal: the eyes looked dusty and pitted, yet from all the readings the armacolite was pure. Enough in just those two small eyes to supply *Voyager*'s needs for months.

In every other feature, the statue looked hauntingly human. Two arms, two legs, ten fingers, and ten toes, clearly visible because the statue wore minimalist shoes, just soles adhered to the bottoms of the feet. The statue's expression was a gentle half-smile made strange by the disturbing filmy eyes. What this balding creature was doing, or what he represented, was beyond Janeway's comprehension. But the entire feeling from the statue was one of a people Janeway felt she might have liked.

So where had they gone? What had happened to an entire planetful of people?

Torres's voice-over softly murmured to the Captain as Janeway watched the tricorder scan of the nearby park and buildings. The entire planet looked pleasant, almost idyllic. The entire place seemed so clean, almost too perfect in many ways. But she had no idea why that fact bothered her.

Janeway glanced up. The bridge crew was working steadily, Paris at the helm, Kim still following the away team's progress. Janeway felt tension in her shoulders and back. The team needed to make it to transporter range.

She hoped they would have time.

The scan wasn't turning up anything she could use in this moment. There was a lot of information that would become part of the archives. But there didn't seem to be anything the away team had missed.

The scan focused in on two buildings and Janeway turned up Torres's voice slightly, but not enough to interfere with the bridge crew's work.

"There seem to be thin wires of armacolite set right in the glass of these structures," Torres's voice said. "I think these people have discovered other properties of armacolite that I'd like to look into further—it's part of their computer architecture, and—"

"One minute to subspace wave," Tuvok said.

Janeway paused, saved the tricorder scan, wishing it had provided more information—the right kind of information—and looked around at Kim.

"Are they clear of the energy interference yet?"

"No, Captain," Kim said without looking up. His fingers moved quickly over his panel. "The landing party has almost made it to the edge of the city, but the energy buildup is just too much. There's no way to break through it with a transporter beam, not reliably or safely, anyway."

Janeway turned to face the forward viewscreen. Something was about to happen on that seductively beautiful planet below, where buildings and streets stood empty, so recently empty that no dust had settled yet. Four of her people were down there in the midst of an energy buildup of an undetermined nature, and even though *Voyager* had weathered a number of these subspace events without consequence, Janeway was worried.

Very worried.

But she had no choice. The away team was just going to have to ride this one out on the surface.

She turned back to Kim. "Ensign. Keep trying right up to the moment of the subspace pulse."

"Yes, Captain," Kim said.

"Mr. Tuvok," Janeway said, "I want every detail of this echo effect recorded again. When this pulse is over, I want to know *exactly* what is happening."

"Aye, Captain," Tuvok said.

"Ten seconds," Kim said.

Janeway turned back to the screen.

The planet below her looked normal, tranquil in its steady orbit. Then a bright, shimmering effect flickered over the entire planet.

Then it all went white.

Pure, blinding white.

Voyager seemed to almost sway in the impact of the wave as it radiated outward.

On the screen thousands of identical planets faded off to the right, dwindling down into tiny blurs of points.

And half the number of *Voyager*s, one in orbit over every second planet.

Janeway sat forward, staring at the images. For over a hundred systems to the left there was no planet. Only asteroid belts and *Voyager*s. Then beyond that the planets started again. Did those images without planets have something to do with the population disappearing?

As quickly as the effect had started, it was over. One could imagine that the white wave had blasted everything on the planet's surface into nothing, but there the planet lay in the gentle light of the sun, sparkle coming from its oceans and clouds, its continents green and gold and ribbed with dark mountain chains.

Again her ship was the only *Voyager* in the sky over a single planet.

Janeway eased back into her chair, staring at it, trying to make any sense out of what she had just seen.

"Captain!" Kim's shaking voice broke the silence of the bridge. "The away team is gone."

CHAPTER
14

Time: The eighty-ninth shift
Location: 2,410 parallel universes to the right
  of ours

THE BOY SHUDDERED AND SHUDDERED, STARED DOWN
at his bruised hands, then up into Kes's face.

Most of the crew had spent the last hour converting cargo bays and holodecks into emergency sick-
bays, but all the real biobeds were in the original
sickbay, and the portable biohealer Kes was using
didn't have much effect on the massive tissue
damage these people had endured. She and other
crew members constantly refilled their hyposprays
with antibiotics and painkillers and went from one
near-dead person to the next, administering medi-
cines as quickly as possible.

Kes's hip pack was full of water pouches. These
people could not drink, their mouths were so
wounded from the attack of vacuum, the explosive
decompression; they were suffering severe dehydra-
tion. She banded the water pouches to their arms,
attaching infusers to seep the water into them
subcutaneously, drip by drip.

Torres had deployed a containment field full of atmosphere around thousands more. Kes shook her head, thinking of those people in that invisible bubble. They were still alive, she had heard from one of the engineers. But how could *Voyager*'s crew take care of them? The crew was at the outer limits of their endurance now, and the ship was straining at its energetic edges providing life support and space for the ones the transporters had managed to bring on board.

Those people in the containment field were out there floating, weightless among the bodies of other dead. They would have no idea how they were even breathing. Or why.

They wouldn't know which way was up or down, or how to go anywhere but where they were.

They would not know what came next, or why they had come here in the first place, anymore than anyone on *Voyager* understood what was going on.

How could they not go mad? Just the thought of it ate at Kes's mind.

The shuddering boy put his hand on Kes's wrist. "Where . . ." he croaked from a raw throat. Blood had coated the skin around his mouth, dried and flash-frozen; his nose and cheeks were brown with blood. His eyes were red with burst capillaries around their dark irises.

Kes stroked his straw-stiff hair. Suddenly she was receiving a kaleidoscopic array of images from the boy, almost as if she were linked with his mind.

Telepathy.

This race must have a subtle telepathy that was

enhanced by this crisis. And she was able to pick it up somehow.

She felt a shudder run through her. She wasn't sure if it was his or hers. For a second, before she was overwhelmed by images, she was relieved that the telepathy was no stronger than this. Imagine being overwhelmed by images of all the dying.

She would lose her mind.

But it wasn't that strong. The images came to her from this boy because she had touched him. Because their eyes met.

She didn't fight the images, letting them flow through her.

Comforting, familiar tunnels, other children joining him as they were on their way to—and then a white flash, and then a horrible weightless shock of disorientation, freezing, lost in floating carnage of gray, bloated bodies, staring into an obviously dead face that even in its distended, bruised state looked like his own.

His breath bursting and blood bubbling from his mouth and nose, his eyes caught in the vice grip of vacuum, eardrums exploding in the sides of his head, and then, suddenly, a shimmering—

He was here, with other people who looked like they had been through a terrible collision, his skin burning and burning, first hot, then freezing cold, his throat an open, grating wound, his stomach queasy; he could still

*remember how his guts had tried to push their
way out of his stomach, like snakes writhing
inside him. And now this young woman with
strange ears leaned over him, brandishing
unfamiliar tools.*

*All his world and everyone he knew was
gone.*

Was he dead?

Was this the Afterworld?

His mind kept echoing with the successive
shocks he had just undergone.

Sense was far from him.

Kes kept her hand on his head, knowing he felt
the warmth of it. "You're on a ship in space. You're
alive. You're safe now," she said gently in her
warm, deep voice.

Her certainty flowed into him, calming his mind-
storm of horrors. "You can sleep now," she murmured. She could sense that the painkillers she had
given him soothed the pain, and her suggestion
made more sense than anything else.

Kes watched the boy slide down and curl into a
ball on the deck. His breathing slowed and his
terrors faded. For a moment she stood there,
watching one small boy out of billions, one small
boy who, for the moment, was content. She narrowed her focus down to this boy.

It was all her mind could hold.

One boy.

Then the sobbing and moaning, the thick smell

of rotted skin and blood, crowded in around her, pushing her back to the reality outside of that one boy.

Everywhere she looked, she saw people in pain, people in shock, people who needed her. She took a deep breath and moved to the next person, a young woman who was barely breathing.

And as she did so, she wondered how many other young women floated in space, how many more would appear? How many dead before this day was over?

How many before *Voyager* lost its capacity to help even one?

How many?

She didn't know, and she couldn't think about it.

The only way she could deal with it was to look at the devastation one victim at a time.

CHAPTER
15

Time: The eighty-ninth shift
Location: Our universe

AGAIN CAPTAIN JANEWAY STARED AT AN ASTONISHING sight in the forward viewscreen: an array of universes stretched into infinity in two directions, with *Voyager*s in half of them. What that meant didn't entirely sink in, although she knew, in some part of her mind, that other Captain Janeways were making every decision she made at the same time. If those other Janeways had made very different choices, their universes would have branched off so radically they would no longer be such a thin wall away. So here they all were, following basically the same path.

She braced herself for the subspace wave, wondering what it was about the light that opened this rift.

There was an answer in this. An answer in everything.

But in the seconds that the rift was open, it made her realize how much of her life was based on small decisions. How much all of the Janeways' lives were based on small decisions. She could have chosen different candidates for various posts: She had come close to choosing a different operations officer, a classmate of Harry Kim's named Daniel Byrd, equally qualified, but with some different skills. She could imagine universes where *Voyager*'s crew and the Maquis never blended into one after their encounter with the Caretaker. Universes where she had stayed on a science career track instead of switching to command.

Universes where each of her crew had chosen differently at major crossroads.

All those *Voyagers*, where major decision trees had rerouted destiny much more radically, were probably not in this visible string of facing images overlapping like cards being shuffled, a sliver of each edge visible past the nearer one in both directions.

These *Voyagers* were closer to her than the others.

And in that she might find some solutions.

She stared at them, at the holes between them, the planets that did not have a *Voyager* in orbit, and allowed herself, in that split second, to remember the one time when she had come face to face with herself:

Voyager had ducked into a plasma drift to avoid a marauding Vidiian ship, and, on emerging, had gone through a divergence field that had seemed to double everything about *Voyager* except for the antimatter.

For a brief time everyone had had a twin, a living, breathing double, only a thin skin of reality away, so close they could establish communication; and one Janeway had crossed through a spatial rift and boarded the other's *Voyager* to confer with her counterpart.

She had looked into her own face. She and her twin had stared at the reality that only one of them could survive this situation, and each of them had been ready to sacrifice her own ship and everyone on it if it would benefit the other. "You know how stubborn I can be," one said to the other. Janeway was no longer certain which of them had voiced it, but she knew both of them had thought it.

Ultimately the decision of which ship survived was prompted by the fact that one ship was invaded and subdued by the Vidiian ship, but not before Janeway's twin had activated the self-destruct sequence.

She had, in effect, outsmarted herself.

She might have to do the same thing again.

And then the three seconds ended. It had felt, for a moment, as if time had stopped.

But it hadn't.

Had it?

Tuvok was leaning over his console. "Now," he said, and she wasn't quite sure what he was referring to, her mind so caught up in alternate universes, the small decisions, the choices that had led her, and an infinity of her counterparts, to this place.

As soon as the word left Tuvok's lips, all the

planets and duplicate *Voyager*s vanished. The subspace wave shook the ship. Rattled it. Made small things bounce.

Why were the small things suddenly so important to her? She was giving herself a message, and she hadn't yet figured out what it meant.

On screen only one planet remained.

"Captain," Ensign Kim said. "The landing party!"

Janeway spun around, small things forgotten. "What about the landing party?"

"They're gone," Kim said. "I've been searching for their location since the end of the pulse and I can't find them anywhere."

This was not small. This was not the change of an eye color, the donning of a new tunic.

She clenched a fist. "Patch me through to R'Lee."

Kim nodded, then looked puzzled. "Captain, they are hailing us."

"On screen," Janeway said.

R'Lee's now-familiar face stared out of the viewscreen at them, but there was something different about him this time. In the brief time since they had last talked with him, just before the subspace pulse, he had changed his blue toga for a gold one, and his silver chain for a black one.

He stared at them, his gray eyes wide in astonishment. He swallowed and said, "Greetings, Captain Janeway. It is good to have you back. We hope you are safe."

"Back?" she glanced around at Tuvok. He gave

no indication that he understood, so she turned to R'Lee. "We have gone nowhere. I just spoke to you a moment ago. Just before the pulse."

R'Lee looked puzzled. He ran a pudgy hand through his tuft of hair. "After our first short conversation, during the pulse, you vanished. We had assumed you were destroyed by whatever is going on."

She let his words come past her, even though she didn't understand them. "The away team? Our crew members you were working with. What happened to them?"

Now R'Lee looked even more confused. "As I said, Captain. You disappeared from our skies during the pulse before this last one. And then appeared again with this pulse. We have not worked with your crew. But we would be most willing to do so."

A chill ran through her. A deep chill.

Small differences.

"Captain?" Tuvok said behind her.

She held up her hand for him to stop. "R'Lee, I must examine our data to see why we're having this difference in experience. I will contact you in a few minutes."

She cut off the transmission without giving him a chance to respond. The image of the beautiful planet again filled the screen. Only this time, just one planet.

But the memory of the string of planets moving off in two directions filled her mind. And *Voyager*s on *every other one*.

She knew exactly what had happened to the away team and her stomach twisted at the thought.

She said, with as much deliberation as she could, "Is there any sign of the away team, Mr. Kim? Any sign at all?"

"No, Captain."

"Is there any trace of them? Anything to show that they were on the surface a moment ago?"

Kim's hand flew across his work surface. "No." He sounded perplexed. "They're not on the surface, and I can't find any trace of them."

"Of course you can't," she said, more to herself than him. She felt a tingle run down her back. She didn't want this to be true. She didn't want to be right, but she was.

"Captain?" Kim asked. "Did they leave the surface?"

"No, Mr. Kim," she said. "They're on the surface. They're just not on this planet."

CHAPTER 16

Time: The eighty-ninth shift
Location: 2,543 parallel universes to the right
of ours

CHAKOTAY WAS A FASTER RUNNER THAN PARIS WAS.

It was irritating. Torres was some kind of speed demon too, Paris thought, watching the engineer as they ran through the empty city streets, trying to put as much distance as possible between themselves and the transporter hub before the next subspace.

Kes was a decent runner, but not a speedy one. Paris, breathing harder than he wanted to, dropped back to run beside the slim Ocampan.

The path they were following was different from the one they had come to the city center on. Paris watched the path when he wasn't glancing sideways at Kes. The purple of the pavement shaded into a pale blue, lightening in color the farther they went. Paris wondered what that meant.

The buildings they were running past looked different too. They were still glass-sided, with wires and what looked like fiber optics running through

113

the glass, but the glass was more peach- and pink-toned, and the rooms inside looked less like family dwellings and more like workspaces. In fact, they were running past one place where Paris saw a conveyor belt with little glass blobs on it. The belt was moving very slowly, dumping the blobs into a pile. The pile was so big it had filled all the available space on into the next room and jammed up against the end of the conveyor belt.

He didn't like this place.

Paris shook his head, then stumbled and fell over a small oval thing that squeaked.

He banged his knee hard, tumbling to stop the rest of the impact. Kes ran on ahead, then turned and saw him rubbing his now-sore knee. She came back and pulled him to his feet. "Are you all right?" she asked in a low voice.

"Fine. I'm fine." Paris watched the little oval robot whirl in a circle and then duck under a curb. He gripped Kes's hand and ran on after Chakotay and Torres. His knee hurt, but not enough to slow him down.

Torres was scanning with her tricorder as she ran. She turned back and called, "I don't think we're going to be able to get far enough out of the energy corona. That subspace pulse will hit in six minutes."

Chakotay slowed to a stop, Torres beside him. Paris and Kes caught up. Paris was winded and tried not to show it, then gave up and took deep breaths.

Chakotay tapped his commbadge. "Chakotay to *Voyager. Voyager,* can you read?"

Nothing but static answered him.

"You don't think it will help if we run another kilometer?" Chakotay asked Torres.

"I don't think it will make enough of a difference," she answered and shrugged. "I wish I'd had time to check out those subway trains. They move a lot faster than we do, but I still haven't seen a way to get down to them."

"Guess we might as well wait it out here, then," said Chakotay.

They had stopped near another of the ubiquitous parks. Chakotay led them over to the grass and they all sat down.

Kes got out her medical tricorder and her bioannealer. "Tom, let me check that knee."

He planted his hands in the short grass behind him, leaned back, and angled his knee toward her. She scanned it with the tricorder. "Nothing too serious, just a big scrape," she said. She took a hypospray from her medkit. "But this might help." She treated him with the hypospray and ran the annealer over his knee. It stopped hurting.

"What happened?" Torres asked with barely concealed amusement.

"I tripped over a robot," said Paris.

"A robot?"

"A little robot about the size of a dinner plate," he said. "It was in the road, and after I tripped over it, it squeaked and ran under a curb."

"Curious," said Torres. She adjusted her tricorder, walked back to the road, and knelt to scan under the curbs. "Hey," she said. "You're right! There's all kinds of concealed machinery here!" She reached in to poke something and a small robot much like the one Paris had tripped over rolled out into the street, chirping angrily at her.

She lifted it to peer at its underside, undisturbed by the increasing frequency of its beeps. "Grumpy beast," she said. She poked a part and it squealed. Then she sighed in disappointment. "Janitor bot."

"What did you expect, a little information bot?" Paris asked.

"Actually, yes," Torres said. "Anything to help us figure out this place." She set it back on the road and it meeped and zipped back out of sight. She picked up her tricorder and stared at it.

Through her serious half-Klingon face, Paris finally understood why she had seemed so disappointed in the bot.

She had seen it as their last hope of getting away from this place before the pulse hit.

"What's going on with the pulse?" he asked softly.

She glanced down at her tricorder again, nodded, and came to sit on the grass beside them. "Well, it's been nice knowing you all," she said.

Chakotay said nothing. Just shook his head.

Paris glanced around. What if the subspace pulses *had* killed everyone on the planet? Killed them so completely not even ash was left? *Were* they about to die? Paris stared at trees, buildings, light blue pavement, clean as a new dawn, unlike any home he had ever had. That was the point, though, wasn't it? Join Starfleet. Seek out new worlds and new civilizations, and eventually die out here among unknown stars?

He just hadn't planned on dying so soon.

But he was prepared for this. They had all been prepared for this, from the moment they entered the Academy.

They all knew the risks.

All except Kes.

The air thickened. The sky shone brighter and brighter, all the blue leaching out of it. Paris closed his eyes against the painful glare, but he could see the light through his eyelids: first red, then pink, then white so white he couldn't see anything at all. He fumbled in the grass beside him until he touched Kes—it turned out he had found her knee, but she closed her hand around his immediately afterward.

He felt a strange lifting sensation, as though he were rising from the ground and floating on a semisolid breeze. For an instant he couldn't feel anything at all, and then sound and touch came back. He felt himself settling to the ground.

Had it even happened?

The light gradually seeped away again. Paris took a deep breath and realized he was still alive. He could smell flowers and grass. And Kes was still gripping his hand. Things could be much worse.

Squinting, he glanced up at the sky. As he watched, it changed from white to pale blue to darker blue, until it matched its earlier color. "We made it," he said, glancing at the others.

"That we did," said Chakotay, one eyebrow lifted as he studied Kes's hand clasping Paris's.

Paris smiled at Kes.

She squeezed his hand and released it. She was comforting him. And all the while, he had thought he was comforting her.

Torres was scanning again. "That pulse discharged all the energy for now." She slapped her commbadge. "Torres to *Voyager*," she said.

Her commbadge emitted slight static.

"Torres to *Voyager*."

The static remained.

Chakotay tapped his commbadge. "Chakotay to *Voyager*."

No answer.

Torres reconfigured her tricorder for long-distance scan. She worked over it for a while, shaking her head in denial of the readings she was getting.

"What is it?" asked Chakotay.

Torres said, "*Voyager* is gone."

Kes paled.

"Are you sure?" Chakotay asked.

Torres frowned ferociously and jabbed fingers at her tricorder, then angled it so he could see the readout. "Gone!" she said. "Not only that, but there is no trace of any warp emissions in this system! It's as if *Voyager* was never here!"

"You have your frying pan," Paris said, "and then you have your fire." He got to his feet. The path—wasn't it a little greener than it had been just a couple minutes ago? He glanced around at the park. Everything looked pretty much the same. One of the trees looked bushier, but how much attention had he been paying before?

"Is this a result of the pulse?" Chakotay asked. "We've been out of contact with *Voyager* for quite some time. Maybe they had to leave orbit."

"The ship was there before the pulse," said Torres. "Nothing can entirely eliminate warp signatures except time."

"Time?" Chakotay asked. "Are there chronoton particles?"

"No more than there were before," Torres said.

"So there were some," Chakotay said.

"There always are," Torres said. "These readings are no different."

"So they didn't travel in time," Paris said, feeling oddly disappointed.

"And neither did we," Torres said. "Something else has happened here."

"I don't think we're going to figure out what it was by standing around this park," Chakotay said. "Let's go back to the transportation hub. Maybe we can figure out how to access those computers. At least we know the pulse originated there."

As they retraced their path, Paris felt the hairs prickling on the back of his neck. Something was seriously wrong here, and it wasn't just the disappearance of *Voyager*. The path was green. It had been blue just a minute earlier. He was sure of it.

But what that meant, he had no idea. None at all.

CHAPTER 17

Time: The eighty-ninth shift
Location: One parallel universe to the right of
ours

"GONE?" CHAKOTAY ASKED.

Paris nodded.

Chakotay pulled out his own tricorder, a movement so fierce that he nearly knocked over a woman who was standing close to him, and scanned.

No *Voyager*.

None.

He closed his eyes, and took a deep breath. The atmosphere in the transporter control room was stifling, even though this place was the size of an arena. Voices murmured around him, and he couldn't think.

Gone.

He opened his eyes.

"Get Kes," he said. "I'll tell Torres."

Easier said than done, it turned out. She was

across the space, and he could feel her anger from this distance. He was afraid she was going to break something.

The chief engineer was steaming, and it was not a good kind of mad. He rose from the computer console a helpful woman had been trying to teach him how to operate, and threaded between colorfully dressed, pleasant-smelling Birsibans toward Torres. Focusing on her anger made his unsettled feeling ease. She was giving him a problem, a *solvable* problem.

Figuring out what caused *Voyager*'s disappearance wouldn't be as hard as calming Torres.

He hoped.

Among Birsibans' civilized murmurs of conversation, Torres's voice stood out, strident and clear. She had grabbed R'Lee by his silver chain and said, "Either you clear all the reporters out of this room, or—"

"Lieutenant!" Chakotay said sharply, but this time she did not respond. Excusing himself, he pushed between people.

"What are these people doing here besides getting in the way?" she cried. She glanced around the transporter control room, which was still clogged with people. The teleconference they had planned to have with transport scientists on another continent had yet to materialize; she had to be reacting to that.

She didn't yet know that *Voyager* was gone.

Chakotay straightened his shoulders, using his

body to force his way through the crowd. A woman touched his arm, and then another did, as if sensing his mood.

They wouldn't really understand. Not even if they had seen what he had on the scan.

Not only was *Voyager* gone, there was no trace of it above them.

No sign that it had ever been there.

Torres was shaking R'Lee by the chain. Chakotay hurried toward her, but couldn't get through the crowd. He wondered if they were about to be arrested and put in jail by whatever passed for police on this world—or possibly even executed. It was a hell of a way to treat the head of the World Council. He gently unclasped both women's hands from his arms and struggled to get closer to the lieutenant.

R'Lee had done nothing to deserve this animosity, as far as Chakotay could tell. His face was red and twisted in a grimace of pain. He grasped Torres's wrists and tried to get her to let go, but she was apparently stronger than he was.

"We have a consensus society," R'Lee said in a choked voice. "It's important that everyone know what's going on, especially during major events."

"How many people does it take to tell the rest of you what's going on? Why won't one reporter suffice?" Torres demanded. Chakotay, still in transit, glanced around, wondering if this assault on a world leader was part of a major event that everyone on the planet needed to know about. Sure enough, a number of people in the crowd were holding up small round palmtop videocams with the lenses aimed toward the world leader and the engineer.

"There are at least three different ways to interpret every situation," said R'Lee. "The superficial, the internal, and the metaphysical; the combative, the inclusive, and the receptive; the—gaahg!"

"Stop babbling and give me a straight answer!" Torres said, jerking the man's chain.

Chakotay had reached them by this time. "Torres, let that man go," he said in his command voice.

"Arrrgh!" she said, and released R'Lee's chain. She turned to Chakotay and glared.

"My apologies, Councilor," Chakotay said to R'Lee.

"Your people are quite different from ours," R'Lee said, rubbing the red chafe marks on his neck. "We don't settle our disputes in such a fashion."

"Er . . . we don't have a consensus society," said Chakotay. "We attempt it. We have many rules about behavior, and we usually try to honor them. Lieutenant Torres usually takes the combative route. She is . . ."

"Exuberant?" suggested R'Lee when Chakotay's pause went on too long. "Energetic? Active? Turbulent?"

Chakotay smiled. He had noticed that R'Lee had a tendency to put the best possible spin on things, and while it led to frustration when they were trying to get a true assessment of events, in this instance it was helpful.

"We are very worried about this strange pulse," Chakotay said. Not an apology for Torres's behavior, but a possible explanation.

She was glaring at him, but some of his concern over *Voyager* must have shown on his face. Her fierceness was fading into curiosity.

R'Lee seemed to take it in that spirit. "I understand. I find it distressing too."

When he spoke, she stopped studying Chakotay. The fierceness that Chakotay thought was gone returned.

"Is there an auxiliary control room," Torres asked, "where there are consoles we can access without all these people around?"

R'Lee looked around him at all the people with news videocams. For a moment he stood, undecided, and then he nodded. "Follow me," he said.

They collected Paris and Kes on their way through the crowd. Kes was speaking softly to Paris. Paris still had his tricorder out, as if the device could make *Voyager* return. Torres looked from one to the other of her colleagues.

She dropped into step beside Chakotay. "All right," she said. "What is it?"

Chakotay nodded to R'Lee. "In a moment," he said.

She understood at once that Chakotay wouldn't speak until R'Lee was gone. He had thought it through in the last few seconds. Chakotay didn't want R'Lee to know the ship had disappeared.

At least, not yet.

R'Lee led them to what looked like a blank gray wall. He stroked a spot on the wall about waist-high to him, and a wide square door popped open. Cool, unscented air flowed from the corridor beyond it, a darkened place with only a few dim lights at irregular intervals along the floor.

"This is one of our access tunnels to the main subway below," R'Lee said. "The new transporter technology was supposed to eliminate our need for these trains. There's a train control station down the hall to the right, and those consoles are still hooked into the planet net." He preceded them into the darkness, tapping the door shut after they had gone through it.

Chakotay looked around as his eyes adjusted to the lower light. The corridor was wide enough for the five of them to walk abreast, though they didn't. He touched a wall, found it cool and textured with small, smooth, discrete tiles in various shapes, some bumpy, some concave, each set into a rubbery-textured fixative. Maybe when the corridor was fully lighted, these walls would display the glory similar to the floor mosaic in the room above.

Maybe not.

No wonder Torres was frustrated. The technology here seemed similar, but was, in fact, quite different.

Paris was still running the tricorder. Torres had

gone to his side and was looking over his shoulder. "Chakotay—" she said.

He held up a hand even as Paris whispered to her, "It's gone. There's no trace."

"There has to be a trace," she said, pulling out her own tricorder.

"Of what?" R'Lee asked.

Chakotay pressed a finger on the wall and the mosaic piece became a dim light. "R'Lee?" he said to distract the Birsiban. "Can you explain this?"

"Eh?" R'Lee came back toward Chakotay. "Oh, you're activating some of the smartglass."

R'Lee ran his hands over the wall, then pressed several small tiles in sequence, and the whole wall lit up, showing swirls and patterns of orange, red, yellow, and brown in translucent, backlit glass.

"Astonishing," said Chakotay. He had the feeling that there was something the pattern was trying to tell him, and he could almost grasp it. The feeling faded swiftly, though, and then he was standing there looking at pretty glass.

Ahead of him, Torres was slapping the side of her tricorder. When it didn't yield the result she wanted, she grabbed Paris's. R'Lee started to look in that direction, so Chakotay said, "What do your people use the smartglass for?"

"It has many uses," R'Lee said. "A think aid, and it can carry out calculations and household operations, maintain environmental controls, access and communicate damage reports from whatever other arrays it is connected to—"

"It's very pretty," said Torres, who had finished

with Paris's tricorder. Her skin had become ashen. She was beginning to understand the situation they were in. "Can we move on? Please?"

R'Lee led them to a room off the corridor. He moved his hands over the wall and lit the room up. Against the opposite wall were more of the same growing-from-the-floor consoles with footwells in front of them that the away team had attempted to examine in the main transporter room.

"I am not skilled in using this kind of equipment, or in instructing others in its use," R'Lee said. "Let me find someone else who is."

"That would be wonderful," Chakotay said before Torres could say what he was afraid she was thinking. "Thank you."

R'Lee bustled off. Chakotay let out the breath he hadn't realized he'd been holding.

"Finally," Torres said in an explosively loud voice.

"You're making this difficult," Chakotay said.

"Me? We don't have time to waste on inanities like making nice with the natives!"

"I didn't want to tell him about *Voyager.*"

"Why not?" Kes asked.

"I'm not sure," Chakotay said. "Just a feeling. I want us to deal with this first."

Torres put her hands on her hips. "Then let's get to it."

"Good luck," said Paris. "I've actually been trying to learn these consoles from someone who knows, and it's counterintuitive. No symbolic representations on any of the touch pads, just colors.

The colors communicate a lot, and I, for one, don't have that particular color dictionary in my head. A lot depends on how many times you tap a particular touch pad, the duration of the touch, and the duration of the pause between touches. None of it comes naturally."

"But that sounds a *lot* like our consoles," said Torres.

"That's part of the problem," Paris said. "The deceptive familiarity. You try to treat these consoles like ours, and see where it gets you. If I had been soloing on one instead of having that woman watching over my shoulder, I could have done a lot of damage."

Torres sat down in front of one of the consoles, tapped her feet down into the footwell. "I'm going to check it out," she said.

Paris shrugged.

"Where's the power button?" she asked. He joined her and tapped a pad on the upper left corner, three short taps. The console lit from within. Torres stared down at the display of colored shapes.

"How much time do we have until the next pulse?" Kes asked.

"Just over an hour, now," said Paris.

"And *Voyager* is gone," Torres said. "How could that have happened?"

Chakotay tuned his tricorder to long-range scan and searched again for their ship. "Not just gone," he said, "but gone as if it had never existed. Not even a trace of warp signature. Nothing."

He thought for a moment. "Maybe that's the answer," he said slowly.

"What?" Paris asked. *"Voyager* didn't exist? Then what did we do, dream it up?"

"No," Chakotay said. "It didn't exist in this universe. And neither did we."

"Don't get metaphysical on us," Torres said. "There must be a simple explanation. A planet-wide shield—"

"On a place with early-warp technology?" Paris asked.

"—or a time fluctuation—"

"I'm not reading an abnormal level of chronoton particles," Paris said.

"—or a delusion of some kind—"

"Or," Chakotay said calmly, "it has something to do with all the other *Voyager*s we saw."

"You mean all those planets fanning out like mirror images?" Kes asked.

"Only," Paris said slowly, "without a *Voyager* in every other universe."

Torres was quiet for a moment. Then she picked up her tricorder. She did a long-range scan. Chakotay watched her. She ran through every system he had thought of, and several he hadn't thought of.

"You're right," she said softly. "There is no trace at all. None. Not even a light-year away. It's as if *Voyager* didn't exist."

"And it didn't, in this universe," Paris said softly.

"I don't like this," Kes said.

Torres snapped the tricorder closed. "So," she

said, "if your theory is right—and that theory seems to be the best we have at the moment—then the entire population of this planet shifted one universe over, us with it. And the population that was here shifted one over, too. And on and on through all the universes."

"That's right," Chakotay said. "It would explain why R'Lee didn't know the Captain after she had talked to him that first time. It wasn't the same R'Lee."

Everyone nodded and silence filled the room for a moment.

"But why are we missing a *Voyager* in every other universe?" Paris asked.

"I'm guessing," Torres said, "but remember when we encountered that plasma cloud and we ended up with two *Voyager*s?"

"And the Vidiians boarded the other one," Kes said.

"And that Captain Janeway destroyed it," Chakotay said.

The group was silent for a moment, all of them following the reasoning.

"Is there a plasma cloud here?" Kes asked.

"No," Torres said. "But I don't think that makes a difference. That event caused a new universe to split from the others, one with a *Voyager* and one without."

"So why so many *Voyager*s?" Paris asked.

"All those represent other events that split off. Any major decision point causes another parallel universe. There are an infinite number of them."

"Okay," Paris said as he put a hand on his forehead. "If we're right—"

"Then the coming energy shift will move us," Torres said, "with the whole population, to yet another planet."

"You mean we'll be two universes away from home?" Kes asked.

"At least there'll be a *Voyager*," Paris said.

"We don't know if we'll go to the next universe over," Chakotay said, "or back to the one we came from. Remember, R'Lee said the changes were slight. I can't imagine they would stay slight if these people are moving from planet to planet like children playing hopscotch."

"These universes have to be similar," Torres said, "for us to be here."

"For *us* to be here, yes," Chakotay said. "The *Voyager*s have to be similar and the difference in each planet would also be small."

"But similar enough to each have this transportation system," Torres said.

"That's just an assumption," Chakotay said. "Maybe, several planets down the line, they didn't activate a system."

"And people are stacking up on some planet like toys on an old-fashioned assembly line?" Paris said.

"That's one possibility," Chakotay said. "But I doubt it would happen. I think we'll go back to the universe we came from."

"It would certainly make things easier," Torres said. But she sounded doubtful.

"Either way," Paris said, "there will be a *Voyager* waiting after the next shift, right?"

Torres only shrugged.

Kes frowned. "And how are we going to tell if we're aboard the right one?"

"Good question," Chakotay said. "Very good question."

CHAPTER
18

Time: The eighty-ninth shift
Location: 2,410 parallel universes to the right
of ours

THE CREW MEMBERS IN THE CONFERENCE ROOM WERE
dead on their feet.

Correction, Janeway thought, breathing deeply
to oxygenate her bloodstream and revive her weary
brain. They had seen enough death; none of them
were dead. They were as tired as people could be
and still be conscious, though.

Glancing at Neelix, Janeway realized that even
that assessment was not universal. The little Tala-
xian rested his head against Kes's as the two sat
side by side. His eyes were closed, and his
breathing—breathing? Call it what it was.

Snoring.

"We all need rest," she said, glancing around at
her senior crew. They looked even more disheveled
than they had before the last subspace pulse.
Everyone on *Voyager* had been working overtime
to take care of the Birsibans—somewhere, somehow, she had discovered that they called their

planet Birsiba, but her mind was so flooded with images, sounds, and smells of the giant floating sickbay *Voyager* had become that she could no longer remember how she had learned this last fact.

They had managed to save four hundred and twenty-eight, a nano-drop from a bucket that held billions of lives. The survivors lay asleep, packed tight against each other, in the converted cargo bays and holodecks and occasionally in crew members' quarters; some even slept along the edges of the corridors.

Four hundred and twenty-eight. Four hundred and twenty-eight shell-shocked souls who needed more food and water and trauma counseling than *Voyager* could provide on a continuing basis. But still, four hundred and twenty-eight who lived.

And her crew members were worn to the edges of their endurance.

They had survivors. She tried to fan the small glow of hope in her heart, but there was too much other smothering news.

They had beamed the bodies of those they could not save out of the ship. They had not had time to do much about those in the containment field besides making sure oxygen was available and placing a highly dispersed, filtered phaser over the mass to make sure there was heat enough in the field to keep people from freezing.

The containment field.

A fact nibbled at the edge of her awareness. A horrible fact.

Tuvok had hypothesized that the only reason the

bodies had piled up in this universe, where there was no planet, was because they were dead, and only living things were shifted by the subspace pulse. What if the next subspace pulse sent all those people in the containment field on to the next universe, leaving the containment field behind? It was a *worse* death than just letting them die *here*. They had spent their last two and a half hours of life terrified, among corpses, in a situation they could not possibly understand . . .

To go on into unmitigated vacuum and there lose life—

She closed her eyes, but she couldn't get the awful visions out of her head. What could they do?

What could they do?

"We have less than thirty minutes until the next shift," Chakotay said. "Another three and a half billion souls are going to flash into space and probably die."

"I know," Janeway said. She rubbed gritty eyes with grimy hands. Too many people had already died, and more were going to die, and she could not control it. Though she put her whole heart into it—though her crew was united in trying to deal with this tragedy—they could not make enough of a difference. Everyone was already worn out. Defeat looked like an option they would have to consider.

She hated feeling so helpless. It was like poison inside her. It reminded her of the time early in her career when she had been locked in a Cardassian prison, listening to the screams of her mentor, Admiral Paris, being tortured while she was powerless to help him. She had never wanted to feel like that again.

She drew in a deep breath, held it a moment, then pushed thoughts of despair away with her exhale. This kind of thinking wasn't getting her anywhere. She straightened. "Does anyone have any answers as to what's causing this?"

Torres shook her head. "We're just seeing the results of something triggered in all the other universes. There's nothing here we can do."

Nothing. She hated that word. Nothing.

And she didn't believe it. There had to be something. Something they could do.

Something she wasn't seeing.

But this problem was too big to handle alone. If only she had more ships.

If only—

She took a startled breath.

She did.

"Captain?" Tuvok asked. For a man who placed no value on emotions, he was exceptionally aware of hers.

"Maybe," she said slowly, "the other *Voyager*s can do something about this if they know about it."

"The other *Voyager*s?" Kes asked. Neelix stirred against her shoulder, but didn't wake up. "Can we contact them?"

"We might be able to," Torres said. "After all, we can see them when the pulse hits."

Janeway nodded to her. She loved it when she and Torres seemed to hit the same thought at the same time. Janeway turned to Harry Kim.

"Mr. Kim, can you get a high speed message to those other *Voyager*s during the three seconds when the universes are open?"

"I think so, Captain," Kim said. "But I'm not sure."

"If we have a tight enough beam, you can do it, Harry," Torres said. "We should be able to get the beam down the line of universes at least as far as our instruments can measure. Maybe much farther."

"All right," Janeway said. "I'll record a message to my counterparts in those other universes. And I want detailed descriptions of what's happening here, as well as full images. I want this message packed solid. Let's get to work. If there's nothing we can do to stop this here, let's drop the burden on the other *Voyager* Captains and see what they can do. This has got to stop."

She stood and for the first time in hours her crew around her felt a little alive. They knew a vast number of souls were going to die in less than half an hour, but at least they were doing something to try to save the next ones.

And the next billions after that.

CHAPTER
19

Time: The eighty-ninth shift
Location: Our universe

JANEWAY PACED THE BRIDGE, OCCASIONALLY GLANCING
at data flowing across the displays behind various
stations. Her away team had vanished; R'Lee—the
third R'Lee—knew nothing, because more than
likely, he'd never seen them. Everyone was working to figure out what was going on during the
subspace pulses. Ensign Kim was studying different sets of information from the scans they had
taken during the last pulse; Ensign Starr was going
over the computer download they had received
from the planetary computers, doing her best to
convert and translate data encrypted in unfamiliar
ways. Tuvok frowned over his console, keying up
displays more rapidly than Janeway could have
comprehended them.

She knew that in Engineering, Lieutenant Carey
and his crew were running calculations, searching
for answers. If this situation could have been

solved by sheer computational effort, they would have had it licked by now.

Obviously, it needed more. She needed fresh insights, extrapolations, ideas.

"Mr. Neelix," she said.

Neelix snapped to attention. He'd been lurking on the bridge since Kes left, peering over shoulders, staring at equipment, but fortunately staying out of the way. Several times she had forgotten he was there, which was different from the past.

He had been standing near Chakotay's station, staring at the viewscreen, but now he had his full attention on her. "At your service, Captain."

She leaned against the railing, hoping her relaxed posture would put him at ease. "Have you seen anything like this before?"

"Which part, Captain?" he asked in his crisp manner.

"All of it," she said. "Any of it." Neelix had proven valuable at times like this in the past. Maybe Neelix had observed something like this before, though he hadn't volunteered any information earlier. Sometimes he was almost *too* forthcoming, but he also had, inadvertently or intentionally, concealed information from her before.

Sometimes it took asking the right questions.

He shook his head. "There've always been rumors of anomalies in this part of space, but to be honest, Captain, I hadn't paid much attention."

Meaning he had never planned on coming in this

direction, so he hadn't thought the information worth storing in his vast detail-filled mind.

"Captain," Tuvok said. "We have ten seconds until the next subspace wave."

She straightened. "I want you to perform a multispectral analysis on this next wave. All of you," she said. "Maybe you'll each see something different."

Tuvok nodded. The rest of the crew bent over their equipment. Neelix continued to lean on the rail, his expression worried.

"People, I need some answers and more than likely we're going to find them during the pulse. Get them." She hoped the missing away team would return during this pulse, but she couldn't count on that. Suddenly, she couldn't count on anything except herself and what remained of her crew.

"Ensign Kim, I want full scans on the planets in the neighboring universes during that opening. If the away team has somehow been shifted over there, I want to know."

"Aye, Captain," Kim said.

Again the planet suddenly spun a cocoon of shimmering white light around itself, and Ensign Kim cued filters on the viewscreen so they wouldn't be blinded.

And then there was that rift between universes, visions of dozens, hundreds, thousands of planets stretching away into two eternities, *Voyager*s stitching through half of their skies.

In the utter silence Janeway heard the small trills

and beeps of the bridge crews' consoles responding to commands. *Collect,* she thought, *gather up everything. Find the clues we need. Give us answers!*

The rift closed like an instant curtain, leaving one lonely planet below them. The subspace wave jolted through the ship.

"Captain," Ensign Kim said. And then, more frantically, "Captain! The away team is on the surface below, right were they were when they disappeared!"

Janeway felt a lift in her heart. She tapped her commbadge. "Transporter room! Four to beam up on my mark. I want them back aboard quickly!"

"Captain," Ensign Kim said, "we also received a high-speed, very compact burst of information through the opening to the other universes. I think it's from another *Voyager,* but it's very faint, as if coming from a long distance off."

"Can you recover it?" Janeway asked.

"I can, Captain," Kim said, "but it's so compact and sent at such high speed that it's going to take me at least ten minutes to reconstruct it."

"Do it," Janeway said. "In the meantime, once the away team is secure, I want all senior officers in the conference room in ten minutes. I want to know what happened for the last two and a half hours."

CHAPTER 20

Time: The ninetieth shift
Location: 2,544 parallel universes to the right of ours

PARIS DECIDED THAT HE HATED THE PULSES, ALMOST AS much as he hated this empty planet. Each time he had been lifted and deposited back on the ground, his eye for color had changed.

The central mosaic tiles in the transportation area had shifted from gold to purple. Now he didn't know a lot about the color spectrum, but he did know that the eye, when faced with gold, did not automatically conjure up purple.

Kes held her medical tricorder over him, and was taking readings. "The pulse seems to have made no physical difference, Tom," she said.

"Then why am I seeing new colors?"

"Maybe for the same reason that this footwell now has places for both feet, where before it was one long unit," Chakotay said.

"The differences aren't just visual?" Paris asked.

"Well, I certainly wish that if things were going

to change," Torres snapped, "they would make this equipment easier to work."

They had spent the last hour and a half underground, below the transporter station, studying the equipment and the holographic globe and anything else they could find.

"What are these people thinking of?" Torres muttered. "A thing is either on or off. Why doesn't it work that way? Where's the sense in this? On, off, maybe-on-off? This is driving me crazy!"

Paris leaned toward her. "I thought you were a wiz at engineering."

She glared at him so fiercely he had to take a step back. Never mess with a Klingon, he reminded himself. Never.

"I *am* a wiz at engineering," she said. "Do you want to try this?"

He held up his hands. "No," he said. "I just want to get out of here."

"Well, Tom, I think someone may have granted your wish." Chakotay was holding his tricorder. "*Voyager* is above us again."

"Fantastic," Torres said. She took out her own tricorder, and then glanced at Chakotay in surprise. "It's as if they were never gone."

"Janeway to Chakotay." The captain's voice sounded tinny and far away in the large space.

The intensity of the relief Paris felt surprised him. Amazing to hear her voice again! He hadn't realized that somewhere inside he had been resigning himself to forging some kind of life on this planet of ghosts, preparing for an uncomfortable inevitability. He turned and grinned at Chakotay, who was smiling just as widely.

"Captain, it's good to hear your voice," Chakotay said.

"Yours too, Commander. How is the team?"

"Everyone is fine, just confused."

"Are you ready to beam up?"

"*More* than ready, Captain."

"I want you up here as quickly as possible, before we have more interference from the energy source. I want a full report in the conference room. I'm initiating transport in five seconds."

"Aye, Captain," Chakotay said.

Torres blew out an explosive breath. "I've never been so glad to hear someone's voice in my life," she said.

Paris glanced around the emptiness, the still-working equipment, the signs of a people suddenly vanished.

"Now that we're leaving," he said, "will at least one of you admit this place is creepy?"

The transporter beam grabbed them before anyone could answer.

CHAPTER 21

Time: The ninetieth shift
Location: 2,410 parallel universes to the right
of ours

THE VISION OF ALL THE OTHER SHIPS, PLANETS, THE
brief stretch of asteroid belts shimmered in the
forward viewscreen for three seconds. Kim's fingers worked furiously across his board, moving
faster than Janeway thought humanly possible. He
knew, they all knew, that the only answer to their
problem—to the problem of billions—lay in getting the message to her counterparts in the visible
universes.

Then the other ships vanished as *Voyager* rocked
with the impact of the subspace wave.

"Mr. Kim?" she snapped.

"The message went through, Captain."

She felt a brief sense of relief, then realized that
sending the message was only the beginning. The
others wouldn't be able to respond until the *next*
pulse.

She was on her own for this one.

Janeway stared at the ominous globe she knew

was composed of billions of dead and dying people. Down inside, below the layers of successive imports of planetary populations, each of which spread outward under power of the momentum the people had had when they were still planetbound in their previous universe, somewhere inside that sphere another planetary population had arrived.

"Torres, what's the status of the containment field?" she asked.

Torres looked up from the engineering station on the bridge. She had come up just before the pulse to help Kim.

"The field is holding," Torres said, working over her console. "But, Captain . . ."

Janeway knew before her chief engineer spoke that her worst apprehensions had been justified. "The last group moved on, didn't they?" she asked in a flat voice.

Kim stared at her from his operations console, eyes wide. Apparently this hadn't occurred to everyone else. Janeway glanced at Tuvok. His grim face gave little away, but through their years of association she had learned to read him. He had considered this possibility, just as she had. Glancing at Chakotay's face, Janeway saw how tight his jaw muscles were.

In a hoarse voice Torres said, "There are new arrivals, but the others are gone."

To their deaths, in a universe without *Voyager.* She had saved them for a death two and a half hours later.

She took a deep breath.

"I was afraid of that," Janeway said. "We must come to a decision on whether to maintain the containment field. What can we do for those people? We couldn't fit any more of them on the ship, and this doesn't seem to be the solution."

"Whatever we do, Captain," Tuvok said, "we must do it before the next pulse."

"I thought of that as well, Mr. Tuvok."

"We can't let them die down there," Paris said.

"What do you expect me to do about it, Tom?" Janeway snapped, even though she knew she should keep a lid on her temper. "Have you any other ideas?"

"No, Captain."

She turned toward Torres. "Maintain the containment field for the time being. Maybe we'll come up with something."

But Torres didn't appear to be listening to her. Her hands were working the console, and she had an expression on her face Janeway had never seen before. "Captain," she said, her voice radiating both astonishment and panic. "I'm reading four Starfleet comm signals coming from the new batch of people in the containment field."

"Ensign Kim, lock onto them and beam them directly to sickbay," Janeway said, rising from her chair and facing Kim.

Starfleet. How did her people get into this mess? Had one of her counterparts sent an away team? Didn't they understand what was happening?

After a moment Kim nodded. "I've got them, Captain. They're in sickbay and all four are still alive."

"Chakotay, Torres," Janeway said, "you're with me." The three of them headed for the turbolift at a run. The nausea she had felt since they had arrived at this hellhole grew even more intense.

She had thought about those myriad *Voyagers* over intact planets, over asteroid belts, wondered who was on them and what actions they were taking in the face of whatever they had found.

If she had sent an away team down to a planet where strange subspace waves rocked reality every two and a half hours, whom would she pick for this assignment? Of course, she was missing a lot of information, like what the situation was on the intact planets. But from what she knew, whom would she send? Would the next captain over have sent the same people? This would be a test of how alike their minds worked.

A very real and important test.

CHAPTER
22

Time: The ninetieth shift
Location: Two parallel universes to the right of
ours

SOMETHING IN THE CONFERENCE ROOM BOTHERED
Chakotay, something small and subtle. He studied
Captain Janeway, who smiled at him, then glanced
around the table at the rest of the senior crew
assembled to hear the away team's report: Neelix,
with an arm around Kes's shoulders—he had
rushed to her the moment the door opened between them; Tuvok, imperturbable as ever; Ensign
Kim, sitting at the conference room console working quietly at something, who smiled at Chakotay
as their eyes met; and the other members of the
away team, Torres, Kes, and Paris.

Everyone looked normal. What was troubling
him?

He was glad to be back aboard *Voyager* after
those unsettling hours on the planet, trying to deal
with helpful people who couldn't seem to grasp
what he needed from them and why. He was

relieved that *Voyager* existed again after that two-and-a-half hour stretch when it had not.

They still hadn't solved the problems caused by the subspace pulse, but at least they were on the ship.

He hadn't been sure that would happen again.

"Boy, it's good to be back," said Paris. He and Kim exchanged grins.

"It is good to have you back," Janeway said. She nodded toward the chairs. Chakotay took his. So did the rest of the away team. "From up here, the problem looks more serious than it did when we sent you to the planet. Your disappearance took us all by surprise."

"Our—?" Paris started, but Chakotay held up a hand.

Janeway shot him an odd look. "Commander? What is going on down there?"

Her crisp manner helped, but didn't make the nagging feeling go away. The nagging feeling that things were different.

Voices kept ringing in his head. Paris and Kes's voices, from just before the last shift.

"Either way," Paris had said about the next shift, *"there will be a* Voyager *waiting."*

Kes had frowned. *"And how are we going to tell if we're aboard the right one?"*

How could he tell? And how much of his discomfort was from his own imagination?

"Commander?" Janeway said again.

"I think the problem is all technological," Chakotay said. He glanced at Torres. She nodded. "And I would prefer to have Torres brief you on that."

Besides, he still needed a moment to reflect, a moment to figure out what exactly had him so on edge.

Torres leaned forward, her eyes bright as they always were when discussing technological matters. "They put a new transport system on line, Captain, and that's when the problems started."

Janeway nodded. Chakotay wasn't sure if she was familiar with that part of the scenario or if she was just encouraging Torres to continue.

"This new transport system is a worldwide grid of interlocking transport beams using a similar technology to our transporters," Torres said. "It is designed to transport everything in designated spaces once every two and a half hours."

"A number of prewarp planets have developed similar technologies," Janeway said. "What's the problem with this one?"

"I don't know," Torres said. "Those people are extraordinarily hard to deal with. I wanted to shut the system down, but even that's not as easy as it sounds. There is no overall on-off switch. Everything down there works in threes, and the master switch for this system—or the master switches, to be more accurate—turn on, off, and do something in-between. By the time I was finally able to convince them to shut the thing off, they told me they had already tried. Nothing stops the system now that it's on."

"That's a problem," Janeway said wryly.

"And there's no fail-safe mechanism?" Kim asked.

"Not that I've found. They didn't seem to understand me when I asked, either." Torres sighed, as if this whole thing were a burden on her. "I was supposed to speak with a team of scientists, but that never happened. I did learn that the system is working automatically now, and that it's drawing thousands of times more energy than is available on the planet. From where, I don't know."

"I wonder . . ." Janeway said. She turned to Kim. "Do you have more information about that vision of the other planets we see during the event?"

Kim nodded. "They actually exist in this universe as well as all the other universes for those few seconds. They are not simply images."

"How is that possible?" Neelix asked.

"I do not know," Janeway said. "What we are apparently viewing is an opening into thousands of other parallel universes that all coexist together on the same plane for slightly over three seconds."

So the captain had come to the same conclusion he had, using different data. Chakotay wasn't sure if that relieved him or distressed him more. He didn't like the feelings he was having.

He didn't like his growing suspicion.

So he concentrated instead on the parallel universes. He thought of them lying face to face like the pages of an antique book, each with its own scripted events, none jumping from one page to the next. Maybe this subspace event was like a spike driven through the book, a corridor that brought all the universes in view of each other.

Massive forces were at work, and they would have to ride them out and deal with the consequences. Consequences like, What was wrong with this room? With his friends and fellow crew members?

"Neelix, when did you cut your hair?" Kes asked, stroking the back of Neelix's neck and looking puzzled.

Well, there was one answer. One difference. But he hadn't noticed it before. Chakotay studied the room and everyone in it, and then, finally, he knew what was wrong.

Their commbadges.

The away team's commbadges had a silver ship over a gold oval. All the crew who had stayed with the ship had gold ships over a silver oval.

The away team was back, all right. Back to a place they had never been before.

Chakotay waited for this revelation to be clear in his head, letting the implications accrue. They were on the wrong ship, in the wrong universe. How much else had changed? What if they couldn't get back to their own ship?

Janeway was still speaking. Only she had returned her attention to Torres. "Is it possible that all those worlds are feeding the system below? And the system below is helping feed the process in all those other worlds?"

"As possible as anything," Torres said. "But that

means to turn it off you're going to have to do so on thousands of worlds in thousands of universes at exactly the same moment."

"Not highly likely," Paris said.

Chakotay could only agree.

A small beep sounded. Everyone frowned, except Ensign Kim, who tapped the screen of the briefing room console.

"Captain," he said. "The message from the other *Voyager* is ready for viewing."

Chakotay was about to lose his moment. He had to speak now. "Pardon me, Captain," he said. "I think there's something we need to discuss before you look at that message."

Janeway's quirky half-smile, the one she always got when she was both saddened and sorry for it, appeared. "I know, Chakotay," she said. "You're not on the right ship."

"What?" Paris asked, sitting up straight.

"That's right," Chakotay said, feeling the first measure of relief he'd felt since he'd stepped into the briefing room. This Captain Janeway was as fast as his Captain Janeway. And that was a very good sign.

CHAPTER 23

Time: The ninetieth shift
Location: Our universe

JANEWAY ENTERED THE BRIEFING ROOM. MOST OF THE staff was already present. Tuvok was seated in his chair, contemplating his hands. Neelix was perched on the edge of his, staring at the door. Ensign Kim was working the briefing console. As she walked past, she noted he was setting up an alarm.

She had just reached her own chair at the head of the table when the away team came in. Familiar faces and yet not familiar. Something about them seemed different.

Small details.

"Boy, it's good to be back," said Paris. He and Kim exchanged grins. A lock of hair hung down across Paris's high forehead. A lock that Janeway couldn't remember seeing before.

"It is good to have you back," Janeway said. She nodded toward the chairs. Chakotay took his. As he did, light glinted off the silver in his hair. Only a strand here and there, with a concentration near his left temple.

She had never noted the strands before.

As the rest of the away team sat down, she made herself focus on the situation. "From up here," she said, "the problem looks more serious than it did when we sent you to the planet. Your disappearance took us all by surprise."

"Our—?" Paris started, but Chakotay held up a hand.

So. To the away team, it had seemed that *Voyager* disappeared. She didn't like the direction in which this was going. Maybe the differences she was seeing were more important than she realized.

"Commander?" she said to Chakotay, allowing him the opening. "What is going on down there?"

He didn't respond at first. He was staring at her, just as she had been staring at him.

As if they were playing in a holodeck distortion program.

As if they were seeing each other for the first time.

"Commander?" Janeway said again.

He seemed to snap to attention. "I think the problem is all technological." Chakotay glanced at Torres. She nodded. "And I would prefer to have Torres brief you on that."

His voice sounded a bit strained, his gaze going to Janeway's hands. She resisted the urge to look at them too. He was glancing at them as if they startled him. As if something were different.

Torres, however, seemed to be her normal self.

She leaned forward, as she often did while discussing technical matters. "Captain," she said, "they put a new transport system on line, and that's when the problems started."

Janeway nodded. She had suspected as much from the information she had received earlier.

"This new transport system is a worldwide grid of interlocking transport beams using a similar technology to our transporters," Torres said. "It is designed to transport everything in designated spaces once every two and a half hours."

Janeway found herself paying far too much attention to Torres's teeth as she talked. There was something odd and different about them. *Focus,* Janeway told herself. The report was more important than the fact that Torres's teeth looked sharper.

"A number of prewarp planets have developed similar technologies," Janeway said, more to keep herself paying attention than to add to the discussion. "What's the problem with this one?"

"I don't know," Torres said. "Those people are extraordinarily hard to deal with. I wanted to shut the system down, but even that's not as easy as it sounds. There is no overall on-off switch. Everything down there works in threes, and the master switch for this system—or the master switches, to be more accurate—turn on, off, and do something in-between. By the time I was finally able to convince them to shut the thing off, they told me they had already tried. Nothing stops the system now that it's on."

In Torres's voice, Janeway could hear the echoes of a deep frustration, even an anger at the way the Birsibans had worked with her. Janeway glanced at Chakotay, who was watching her closely. He must have had a handful on that planet.

"And there's no fail-safe mechanism?" Kim asked.

"Not that I've found. They didn't seem to understand me when I asked, either." Torres sighed. The sound was not relaxed, but a venting of anger. "I was supposed to speak with a team of scientists, but that never happened. I did learn that the system is working automatically now, and that it's drawing thousands of times more energy than is available on the planet. From where, I don't know."

A thousand times more.

A thousand times.

More.

Janeway flashed on a sudden image of planets, stretching into eternity. "I wonder," she said, and then realized, from her crew's reaction, that she had spoken aloud.

She turned to Ensign Kim. "Do you have more information about that vision of the other planets we see during the event?"

Kim nodded. "They actually exist in this universe as well as all the other universes for those few seconds. They are not simply images."

A thousand times. Janeway frowned. As she did so, she saw Kes touch Neelix's neck slightly.

"Neelix, are you all right?" she asked softly, so

softly that Janeway wouldn't have been able to hear if she hadn't been listening.

So things were different to the away team too. Chakotay's silver hair, Paris's new hairstyle, Torres's teeth were all small differences, yes. But important in their accumulation.

Just as R'Lee was telling them when they had responded to his distress call.

Janeway now knew why the poor man had seemed so unsettled. It was almost more difficult to acknowledge the small differences than it would have been larger ones. She hadn't realized how much details could set her on edge.

And how much they could tell her.

This was telling her that one of her greatest fears had occurred.

The group of people before her was not her away team. This was another *Voyager*'s away team. More than likely two ships over in the string of *Voyager*s.

A small beep sounded. Ensign Kim's alarm had gone off. Everyone frowned, except Ensign Kim, who tapped the screen of the briefing room console.

"Captain," he said. "The message from the other *Voyager* is ready for viewing."

Chakotay looked up at Janeway as if the world were about to end.

He had obviously come to the same realization she had.

"Pardon me, Captain," he said. "I think there's something we need to discuss before you look at that message."

"I know, Chakotay," she said. "You're not on the right ship."

"What?" Paris asked, sitting up straight.

"That's right," Chakotay said. He sounded both startled and relieved.

"We'll deal with that in a moment," she said, putting off the question of what to do until she had a few more minutes to digest the implications. "Let's see what the other captain has to say first. Perhaps she knows more than we do."

Janeway brushed away a loose strand of hair, then swung her chair toward the viewscreen. "Mr. Kim, put the message on screen here."

Kim tapped a control, and Janeway's own image appeared on the conference viewscreen. She had seen herself before—once in person, and all of her life as mirror and recorded images. But in each of those images, she remembered looking the way she had. She remembered the actual recording.

But this time, she felt the hairs on the back of her neck rise. The Janeway before her wore clothing that this Janeway had never seen. The recorded Janeway wore an orange and black uniform instead of a red and black one, and her hair was wrapped in a braided coronet about her head. She looked exhausted; a few stray tendrils of hair drifted down about her neck, and her eyes were sunken.

Something terrible had happened to her.

Something that had not—yet—happened here.

"Captains of *Voyager*," the Janeway on the screen said, her voice raspy with fatigue, "I'm assuming that many of you have figured out what is happening on whatever planet you are orbiting, but I must show you the full scope of this disaster. In the universe we inhabit, the planet you now orbit was somehow destroyed."

A visual of an asteroid belt flashed on the screen. The sun it ringed looked just like the sun in the Birsiban system.

Then new Janeway came back on screen, staring at the briefing room as if she could actually see it.

Maybe she had seen it.

In her imagination.

"Actually," the recorded Janeway said, "this world was destroyed in one hundred and thirty universes. For ease of communication, I will say that those universes exist to my right as I face the main viewscreen and the images of all the universes during the subspace event."

Another visual took her place, showing the image while the universes were open during the subspace disturbance. For a distance there were no planets, only *Voyager*s above every second asteroid belt. Then in the distance the planets were again whole.

The recorded Janeway spoke again. "However, my ship is in one very *unique* universe. We are orbiting a debris field in the universe closest to the last intact planet universe, to what I am calling my left."

"Freeze visual," Janeway said. She glanced around the table. "Is everyone following this?"

"How, if these universes are parallel, can something be different on over a hundred of them?" Neelix asked.

"Take a look at Kes's face," Janeway said. "Notice the difference?"

Neelix swallowed. "Her skin tone is slightly darker, but I thought that was due to the effects of Birsiban sun."

"That, and her thinking your spots are bigger?"

"Or the fact that you're no longer wearing your good-bye ring from Mark," Chakotay said to Janeway.

Paris was nodding.

"Small differences," Janeway said, "but they exist."

"The farther away we get from our home universe," Torres said, without her usual energy, "the greater the differences may seem."

Chakotay was nodding.

"A large asteroid might have impacted the planet in those universes, where in all the others it missed, or didn't hit in the right place to destroy the planet," Janeway said.

"The difference only needed to be slight," Kim said.

Neelix stared at Kes for a moment, then moved away slightly.

Kes only smiled at him.

"Continue playback," Janeway said. Kim touched his panel, and the Janeway on the screen went on.

"The subspace waves that I assume attracted us all to this system are having a tragic effect," the Janeway on the screen said.

The recorded Janeway took a deep breath.

Watching, Janeway in the conference room took a deep breath as well. Whatever came next would be almost unbearable; she could tell by the way her counterpoint's mouth tightened at the corners.

"Please brace yourselves," the Janeway on the screen said. A moment later an image of a gray, somewhat flattened, planet-sized shape appeared, floating in space where the planet was in most universes. Parts of the flattened sphere were dark, as if something monstrous had bitten chunks from it. Janeway found herself leaning forward, straining to see what the shape was made out of.

"This is my universe," Janeway on the screen said. "What you are seeing is a massive graveyard."

The image enlarged in jumps until it became clear that the shape was made up of humanoid bodies floating in space, clustered thickly in some areas and less dense in others.

"Every two and a half hours, the entire population of the planet in the universe to our right is shifted to this universe, where there is no planet."

The image of Janeway came back on the screen. "Three and a half billion people are dying an ugly death every few hours. We must stop this."

She took a deep breath. "Since I have no planet to work with here, only the disastrous results, I'm asking that the ten *Voyager*s in the universes to my right and the ten over planets to the left work to come up with ideas on how to stop this. Send the ideas to me during the next subspace disturbance."

Again the Janeway on the screen took a long, deep breath. "I'm assuming it will take as many *Voyager*s as possible, in all the universes, working together, to stop this, so I will be the one to send off the results to every *Voyager* my signal can reach. That way we can avoid the obvious confusion of all of us coming up with the same idea and sending it at the same time."

She looked as if she were drawing on reserves that were nearly gone. "We *must* find a way to stop this. I will be awaiting your responses."

The screen went dead.

A shocked silence filled the conference room as the thought of that many people dying slowly worked its way into the brains of the *Voyager*'s crew.

Janeway stood. She couldn't sit still after receiving that information. "Which universe did that message come from? How far from us is she?"

"That ship exists two thousand, four hundred and ten universes to the right, using her measuring system," Ensign Kim said.

"And how many pulses have there been so far?" Janeway asked, not sure she wanted to hear the answer.

Kim bit his lower lip, almost as if he didn't want to let the number out of his mouth. "Ninety."

The number of deaths couldn't register in Janeway's mind. A planet's population had died, not once, not twice, but ninety times.

Ninety times several billion. She wasn't thinking of an abstract number.

She was thinking of living, breathing beings.

No wonder her counterpart had looked so devastated.

Solving this problem in a universe with no planet and one starship was impossible.

It would require a miracle.

Which was what the recorded Janeway was asking for help in creating.

They had less than two hours to prevent billions more from dying.

Janeway clenched her fists.

This had to stop.

And it had to stop now.

CHAPTER
24

Time: The ninetieth shift
Location: 2,410 parallel universes to the right
of ours

KES FELT A SHIMMERING COLD IN HER STOMACH. SHE
was staring down at herself on a biobed.

Around her in sickbay, many of the rescued
Birsibans slept against the walls, leaving narrow
walkways for her and the Doctor to use. In the
Doctor's office, the sick covered the floor completely. They slept under whatever blankets Kes
had been able to scrounge from ship's stores. The
air was still heavy with the scents of blood and
rotting skin. Life support was doing the best it
could to circulate enough air for everybody aboard,
but gone was the pure, almost scentless air they
usually enjoyed.

The survivors with the most physical damage
were in intensive-care containment fields on biobeds.

Four of the biobeds were occupied by the new
arrivals, although none of them had needed the
intensive-care containment fields. The new arri-

vals, Torres, Paris, Chakotay, and this new Kes, had been fortunate enough to end up in the containment field Torres had established in space, where the largest number of humanoids were being shifted. They had been pulled from it quickly, and had apparently sustained no physical damage.

Although Kes didn't know what kind of emotional trauma they suffered, her counterpart looked stunned. Kes could only imagine what the new Kes was feeling. To arrive, suddenly, in the vacuum of space, surrounded by dead bodies, and other living beings, to experience no gravity, and yet to be able to breathe. . . .

How inexplicable.

How terrible.

The new Chakotay seemed to be doing all right, although he kept his lips pressed so tightly together they had turned white. No matter how much training someone had, nothing could prepare him for the horror Chakotay had found himself in.

Nothing.

And things weren't much better on this ship.

Kes wiped an arm over her grimy face. She hadn't had time to clean the blood off. Her clothing stuck to her, and her hair was oily with dirt and filth. She didn't know how many hours she had been toiling on this transformed ship. All she knew was that everything she had done was not enough.

The new Paris was, typically, observing everything from his biobed. He too had a haunted look around the eyes, but he always managed to bury his darker emotions under a surface geniality, and he seemed to be attempting that now.

Kes shook her head slightly. Her Paris did that. This new Paris apparently did too.

The new Torres, whom the Doctor was examining at the moment, was restless, as usual, wanting to get moving, asking constantly what had happened.

Kes's double reached out a hand. "Is this *Voyager?*" she asked.

Kes took the offered hand. It felt like her own, only the angle with which she held it was wrong. And she couldn't feel the pressure of her own hand. Odd to feel the shape and not anything else. Even the new Kes's skin felt the same as hers.

"Yes," Kes said.

"But you're me," the new Kes said. Her voice was shaking.

"No," Kes said. She looked at her bloodstained hand clutched in the new Kes's clean one. "No, I'm not you. Not quite."

She swallowed. How to explain this to a woman who had just gone through one of the worst experiences of her life? An experience that might get worse?

"Remember that plasma cloud?" she asked.

"Oh, yes," the new Kes said, and her eyes drifted slightly to the side, as Neelix said that Kes's did when she got lost in a memory. The memory grabbed Kes too, briefly. She had come face to face with herself before, from the other direction, looking up from a biobed at her medical technician self.

The first time she had encountered herself, *Voyager* had hidden in a plasma drift and come out through a divergence field that doubled everything in the ship except the antimatter. Kes, on her way to help an injured crewman near a hull breach, had slipped through a spatial rift onto the parallel *Voyager,* where she was taken to sickbay.

Then she had found herself staring up at another self. And she remembered how alien it was, as if the face in the mirror had suddenly grown flesh and blood.

Only this had to be worse. Much worse. She didn't look like a mirror reflection. She knew she looked like someone who'd been through a war zone.

"What's happening here?" the new Kes asked.

"Lieutenant," the Doctor said both loudly and crossly to the new Torres, "you're not going anywhere until I've completed my preliminary scans, so you may as well save your energy."

The new Kes had turned her head in the direction of the Doctor's voice. She seemed relieved to see Torres.

"I am fine, I tell you," Torres said.

"I'll be the one to say who's fine and who's not," the Doctor snapped. "As long as you're in my sickbay, you will do as I say."

"Nothing has happened to me. We had air, which is more than I can say for some of those poor souls. Now tell me what's going on here, or I'll—"

"Torres." Chakotay sounded tired. "Let the Doctor finish. He has a lot of other patients."

Torres started to get off the biobed, and the Doctor pushed her back down. "You should see to the others," she said sharply.

"I *will,*" he said. "As soon as I'm finished with you."

"This is blackmail," she muttered, but she didn't move.

The new Kes shifted uncomfortably, and turned her attention back to Kes. "How come there's only one of them, and two of me?"

"There's two of them," Kes said. "Just not in sickbay."

"Kes?" Paris said from the biobed behind her.

"Yes?" Kes and the new Kes turned to look at him.

His eyebrows rose in confusion. "I'm seeing double."

Kes smiled at him. "Not exactly," she said. She half-turned back to the new Kes so she could speak to both of them at once. "We believe you jumped from one universe to the next beside it."

"What?" asked Paris. "But that doesn't—"

The sickbay door slid open and Captain Janeway, Chakotay, and Torres strode in. The captain's hair had completely fallen out of its usual corona at the top of her head. The braid trailed down her bloody uniform, hair pulling out of it. She had dirt on her face, and shadows beneath her eyes so deep that her eyes nearly disappeared.

Chakotay looked a little better only because his hair was cut so short. His face was streaked with blood and his uniform was torn in three places. His mouth had formed a line so straight that it looked as if he might never smile again.

Only Torres still seemed to have a bit of energy left. It was her Klingon self, all focus and determination in the face of adversity. Somehow it seemed to give her more reserves. She was coated in grease and oil and she had a dark patch of something— blood? dirt?—on her chin.

Chakotay's eyes widened as he stared at the new Chakotay on a biobed, who was also watching him with surprise. Kes glanced from one to another and saw something different: The new Chakotay's tattoo showed a small spiral line near the edge of his left cheek, with a ray of lines fanning from it up a fourth of the way across his forehead. Chakotay's tattoo was a circle on his upper left cheek with an equal-armed cross in it.

Torres strode to the biobed where the new Torres lay. Her mouth hung half-open as she stared down at herself. The new Torres frowned up at her.

"Ohhh, man," muttered Paris from the bed behind Kes. "Is there one of me here too?"

Kes nodded without turning toward him.

"You're the away team?" Janeway asked.

"Aye, Captain," the new Chakotay said. Then he blinked, stared at his twin, and shook his head as though to clear his vision. "What—"

Chakotay only shrugged.

"I'll explain in a moment," Janeway said. "Doctor, how are they?"

"I am still finishing my evaluation, Captain," said the Doctor in an irritated voice, running a medical tricorder over Torres's forehead. "Why are you people so bad at following your doctor's orders? I'm not in the habit of making frivolous suggestions." He paused to glare down at the new Torres, who raised her eyebrows at him.

After a moment the Doctor turned to face Captain Janeway. "It appears that they have not suffered any major physical distress."

"Good."

He glared at each of his new patients, then sighed. "You're free to go," he said, "but I would suggest that you take things easy. You've had quite a shock."

The new Torres sat up immediately and pushed away from the bed, keeping some distance between herself and Torres. They studied each other with narrowed eyes.

"Not, of course," the Doctor continued, "that you'd listen to me."

Chakotay held out a hand to the new Chakotay, which was clasped. They stood for a moment, studying each other, hand gripping hand. Paris got up and rubbed the back of his head. "Am I going to meet myself?" he muttered to Kes.

"Probably," she murmured back.

"Boy, I don't think I'm ready for this," Paris said. He shook his head. "Can't look myself in the face most mornings as it is."

"Don't worry, Tom," both Keses said at once.

"Ouch! Don't do that!" said Paris, holding his head.

Kes let go of the new Kes's hand and they

separated. They were both grinning at Paris, and when they noticed, they stopped. Kes remembered this feeling from the first time she met with herself: the awkward familiarity, and the matching discomfort.

"Do you need Kes right now?" The captain was asking the Doctor. "I'd like her to attend the briefing as well."

"The situation appears stable," he said, glancing around. Everyone besides the crew and the new crew was sleeping. "Unless you're planning to stuff more people onto this ship."

The captain put a hand to her messed hair. "I don't know what I'll do, Doctor. But for the moment, there will be no new patients."

"Unlike the others," he said, "I don't need to rest."

"I know," the captain said, "but we've already strained this ship to capacity."

She glanced around sickbay as if it were someplace new. Kes watched her, knowing the feeling. Kes had never seen so many people here.

So many innocent, dying people.

"If nothing changes in the next few minutes, Doctor," the captain said, "we could use your on screen presence at the briefing as well. Although I do think you'd better stay in sickbay for now in case of emergencies."

"I quite agree, Captain," said the Doctor.

Janeway tapped her commbadge. "Senior officers to conference room one," she said, and started for the door.

"Excuse me," the new Kes said. "Does that include us?"

The captain's smile was gentle and understanding. "Yes, it does, Kes. Are you up for it?"

The new Kes nodded and sat up. "I would love to have something to do," she said.

Kes could understand the feeling. But she knew, as the others did, that there was more than enough to do.

The captain looked at the others in sickbay. "Please join us, away team," she said. "We need to find solutions."

Torres was staring at the new Torres, the air between them crackling with barely concealed hostility.

The captain seemed to note that as well.

"And I need everyone working together," she said. "Right, Lieutenant?"

Torres sighed and backed away. "Sure, Captain."

"At least you know that my observations will be good ones," the new Torres said.

"I don't know anything," Torres responded.

"That makes two of us," Paris muttered as he stood.

"Three," Kes and the new Kes said in unison. And then they looked at each other, startled, and laughed.

It was all Kes could do. If she let any other emotion out, it would be tears.

And weeping wasn't a luxury any of them could indulge in for some time to come.

CHAPTER 25

Time: The ninetieth shift
Location: Our universe

TOM PARIS RETURNED TO HIS SEAT AT THE HELM. ONLY it wasn't his seat. The chair was a centimeter too high. His knees knocked against the console. How did his counterpart, the Paris from this universe, handle the discomfort?

Or was that Paris slightly shorter?

The captain hadn't yet arrived. She was going over some engineering information with Torres. Harry Kim had come with Paris to the bridge, and then had gone immediately to his station.

No banter.

No welcome back.

Paris turned in his chair. Except for Ensign Starr and Chakotay, he and Kim were the only two people on the bridge. And Harry hadn't said a word to him.

"I don't bite, Harry," Paris said.

"I have to finish this," Harry said, head down.

Harry had never treated him like this before.

Usually there would have been some banter, or some conversation between them. But since they'd left the briefing room, Harry hadn't spoken to Paris at all.

Paris stood, banged his knees, and stifled a curse. Of all the regulations, the ones he broke the most had to do with proper use of language. Even though, he suspected, every stiff-necked admiral of every fleet would allow him a curse or two at this point in his life.

Paris crossed the bridge and stopped below Harry's station. "Harry," he said.

"Tom," Harry said, his mouth so tight the word came out strained. "I have to do this. Billions are dying."

"I know," Paris said. "But usually you and I work well together. It would be bad for the bridge crew to have something going on between us."

Harry brought his head up. "You don't know how 'you and I' normally work."

Paris stared at him a moment, feeling a flush rise in his cheeks. He could either sit back down like a good little stranger or he could establish his own place in this new universe. In a universe he might have to spend the rest of his natural life in.

"If I had treated you like this, Harry, when you had come from the other *Voyager,* think how different your life would be," he said.

Harry's face went completely blank. Paris suddenly realized he'd struck a nerve.

"That's what's going on, isn't it?" Paris said.

"*You* don't feel like you belong, so you're going to make me feel unwelcome."

"I belong," Harry said. "The *Voyager*s hadn't spent any time apart yet."

"But you lived a different last hour from your counterpart," Paris said.

"But I wore my hair the same," Harry said. "I didn't expect an easy relationship with everyone on board."

"Although they gave it to you," Paris said. "Although *we* gave it to you."

"Yes," Harry said. "You did."

Paris grinned. "There," he said. "You've accepted me. So lighten up."

Harry frowned. "What? I haven't done anything."

"Oh, but you have," Paris said. "You said that we accepted you."

"You did," Harry said.

Paris shook his head. "I accepted another Harry Kim," he said softly. "Two universes over."

Harry groaned. He brought his head down slightly. "Tom—"

"It's nothing, Harry," Paris said, hearing the conciliation in Harry's voice. "We are who we are. We may be slightly different, but we're the same people inside. And that's why people on every *Voyager* in all the visible universes accepted you with no questions asked."

"All of them except me," Harry said. "I didn't accept me."

"I can relate to that one," Paris said, and returned to the helm. He hit his knees again and winced. How many conversations were Tom Parises having with Harry Kims on how many *Voyagers*? And how many still felt as unsettled afterward as Paris did?

Because, if he were honest with himself, he was reacting just as Harry had. This wasn't his *Voyager*. These weren't *his* people.

But they were close.

And that counted for something.

He paused, hands over the console.

It had to count for something.

This *Voyager* was all he had.

CHAPTER 26

Time: The ninetieth shift
Location: Our universe

JANEWAY STEPPED OFF THE TURBOLIFT AND ONTO THE bridge. Torres was beside her. They had spoken briefly after the meeting. Janeway had wanted to see if this new chief engineer was significantly different from the old one.

In temperament they were exactly the same. There were minor differences, but Janeway didn't think they would affect Torres's performance.

She wasn't yet sure of the rest of the new away team.

The bridge crackled with the residue of tension. Chakotay had moved to his usual post. Ensign Starr was working in her area, seemingly undisturbed. Harry Kim was bent over his station, cheeks flushed. Tom Paris, the new Tom Paris, was sitting at his console, hands paused above it as if he wasn't sure how it worked.

"Do the controls look familiar?" Janeway asked as she went to her command chair.

Paris snapped out of his momentary funk. He stared down at his helm console, running a touch too light to activate anything across the control pads. Most of them weren't labeled. "Unless there's a monkey wrench in here somewhere, I should be fine," he said.

Kim's flush grew darker. What had they discussed?

She didn't have time to find out.

The turbolift doors opened again, and Tuvok came to the bridge. Neelix and Kes followed him, even though they would have little to do.

"I may need you in sickbay, Kes," Janeway said. "Why don't you go below and see if things are as you remember them?"

Kes put her hands behind her back. "That's a good idea, Captain," she said. Her startlingly deep voice was the same, and so were her movements. Yet Janeway knew, on a gut level, that this was not the Kes she had known for the past few years.

"I'll go with her," Neelix said.

Janeway wasn't sure that was a good idea. Neelix and Kes had been close. Neelix would notice the differences more than some others would.

"I need you to continue your tasks as morale officer," Janeway said. "I suspect most of us won't get any sleep while we're handling this crisis. Make sure that food is available so that we can keep our energy up."

"Aye, Captain," Neelix said, even though he sounded unhappy about the duty. He followed Kes to the turbolift.

Janeway looked at Chakotay, still not used to the strands of silver threading through his hair. "Is everything as you expected?"

"More or less," he said. "The differences are slight and subtle, but not unworkable."

"Is that the same for you, Torres?"

Torres had taken her place on the bridge, the one she usually had when she wasn't in engineering. She studied the science station for a moment. "I see no problems, Captain."

"Good," Janeway said. Having her senior crew back in positions would be more helpful than not, even though they weren't exactly her crew. She turned to Kim. "Have you been able to combine our records with the records from that message?"

"Aye, Captain," Kim said. His flush had receded.

"Can you put the exact location of the message's *Voyager* on screen?"

Kim nodded and worked his board. After a short moment he said, "Here it is, Captain."

The image of the planets disappearing off into the distance filled the main screen. Kim, using the computer to extrapolate the images, pulled the viewpoint above the planets as if *Voyager* had left orbit and had moved far out into the system. The planets stretching into the distance became nothing more than a long line of dots on the screen, broken only for a short distance. It was at the beginning of that break that Kim focused the image.

"That *Voyager* is two thousand and ten universes

away, Captain," Kim said. "Our readings corroborate what . . . the other Captain Janeway . . . the one on the screen, said."

Janeway stared at the image before her. The thought of all the populations of all those planets being shifted into the cold of space made her head spin. Billions of humanoid lives lost every few hours. It would take only about five thousand hours before every life on the planet below them now would be shifted to that universe without a planet and killed.

"Okay, people," she said, turning to her crew. "We need to figure out how to stop this carnage. The people below have asked for our help, so we're not going to violate any Prime Directive. And to be honest with you, with this many being killed, I wouldn't care if we were. I want a solution."

Everyone nodded, but no one spoke up. The answers weren't easy.

She wished they were.

"Second," she said, "we need to come up with a way to return this away team to their own ship, and get our team back."

"I feel so unwanted," Paris said, smiling up at her.

"No offense, Mr. Paris," she said, smiling back, glad he was here, even if he wasn't the Paris she was used to. She had forgotten how much she counted on his wry comments to lighten the mood on the bridge.

"I suspect," she continued, "that in solving the first one, we will solve the other."

"I hope so," Chakotay said softly.

Janeway ignored his comment. She did have a few ideas of her own. Right now she wished she had fewer captain's duties, and could concentrate on applied science. It would take all the scientific knowledge they had to save even half of the lives before them.

"Lieutenant Torres," Janeway said, "would it be possible to get a transport beam through the opening in the universes?"

Torres nodded. "Theoretically, yes. From everything we can tell, the universes are actually hooked together in that opening during those few seconds. If that other *Voyager* could get a message through, we should be able to perform a transport."

"Are you thinking of transporting everyone back to their proper universe, Captain?" Paris asked, sounding skeptical.

"It would work only if all ships occupying these thousands of parallel universes did exactly the same thing at exactly the same time," Tuvok said. "The probable chance of such an event occurring is—"

"Not relevant at the moment, Tuvok," Janeway said. "I'm not sure we have the energy to handle such a plan. I simply wanted to know if our transporter would work across universes. And if it can, as Lieutenant Torres says, we have a weapon in our arsenal."

All she really wanted to do was to get her crew thinking in more than one dimension. For three-point-two seconds every two and a half hours, they had the power of not one, not two, but thousands, maybe millions, of *Voyager*s. That had to count for something.

"Lieutenant," Janeway said, "you've seen their equipment. Do you have any ideas as to what might stop that reaction below?"

"Not yet, Captain," Torres said. "I'm not even sure where all the extra energy is coming from. Or why it only takes humanoids, and not everything else, including the planet itself."

Janeway nodded and stared at the image on the screen. She felt the same frustration that Torres's words expressed. Were all the Janeways, in all the universes, right now feeling the exact same thing?

She shook the thought away and turned back to Torres. "Would full destruction of their transportation system and energy storage system stop this?"

"No," Torres said. "I did look at that option when I was below. As I said, there, the lack of a failsafe makes this system self-perpetuating. It's as if the energy is controlling the machine rather than the machine controlling the energy. Plus, I doubt this is contained inside their machines. This seems bigger."

"But something has to cause the system to work together," Janeway said. "Something enables that machine and that energy to work together."

"I'm sure there is," Torres said. "But I haven't found it. And even if I do, I'm not sure we have enough force to stop it."

Janeway peered at her. "How about the force from thousands of *Voyagers*?"

Torres glanced at the captain, catching what she was thinking. "Possibly."

"Excellent," Janeway said. "Now all we have to do is find the right target."

CHAPTER
27

Time: The ninetieth shift
Location: 2,410 parallel universes to the right
of ours

JANEWAY'S READY ROOM NO LONGER LOOKED LIKE THE
peaceful retreat it had once been. The flowers Kes
had placed on her glass table had been shunted to a
corner. Now there were padds, confidential materials, and bandages covering the table. Boxes and
storage equipment had been moved into one corner, as had most of her furniture. She had designated that this room, the bridge, and engineering
remain clear of wounded.

Those were the only places on the ship without
injured people lining the walls, covering the floor,
moaning on furniture.

The only places where the horror of the last few
hours was a slight distance away.

Very slight.

The others didn't seem to feel the respite either.
Her senior officers had pulled chairs into the ready
room, since the briefing room was yet another
auxiliary sickbay. They had crammed into the

remaining space, setting up their chairs as if there were a conference table in front of them. The staff was in its usual position, except for the newcomers, the second Torres, Chakotay, Kes, and Paris. They were different, not just for their slight changes in physical appearance, but also for their cleanliness. They looked a bit shell-shocked, yes. Who wouldn't be after their experience? But they weren't blood-covered, exhausted, and filthy despite their best efforts.

Janeway put a hand on the back of her chair, and surveyed the group, wishing, for half a second, that another Janeway was on board. Then she could work in concert with herself as she had done during the crisis they encountered in the plasma cloud. Only this time, she would have one of her selves working on the applied science problems, and the other self take care of command.

Only the new away team was watching her. The others were slumped in their chairs, taking the few seconds of silence as an opportunity to rest. She found it interesting to note where the newcomers had ended up. The Parises had eyed each other warily, then turned away, almost in unison, as if they didn't want to deal with each other at all—not even think of each other.

The two Chakotays had nodded at each other. The new Chakotay had waited while the other took his accustomed place, then the new Chakotay had taken one of the available chairs, careful not to sit in any original crew member's spot.

The two Keses were probably the most comfortable with each other. They sat near each other, as if they were drawing support from each other. Neelix had taken one look at both of them and taken a different chair. Apparently he was the one who would have trouble with two Keses, not Kes herself.

The biggest problem, though, was with the Torreses. Torres was not comfortable in her own skin. Being faced with another version of herself seemed to be almost more than she could tolerate. The two women had growled at each other as they passed, and neither had made any conciliatory gestures.

They sat at opposite sides of the room.

Torres's inability to cope with another Torres upset Janeway the most. Those were the two who had to work together. If both of their powerful minds were focused on solving this problem, then *Voyager* might have a chance at changing the course of the crisis before them.

If the Torreses did not get along, then they could destroy everything.

Janeway sighed softly and took her chair, officially starting the meeting. She was the one who had to order the Torreses to work together. And if they didn't, she would have to force them.

And she would.

They were running out of time.

She brushed a strand of hair out of her face. It felt odd not to have a table in front of her.

"First," she said, "let me establish some communication protocols. Since we have two people with the same name in four of our positions, we will need a way to refer to each of you. For ease of communication, the newly arrived away team will add a "two" behind their names. Thus the Chakotay sitting in the back of the room becomes Chakotay-two, and so on."

Torres-two turned her head away, as if she were angry but knew better than to voice it. Kes-two looked down at her hands. Chakotay-two did not move. Neither did Paris-two. But she could see the displeasure in their eyes.

"I'm sorry if this seems somewhat demeaning," she said, "but with billions dying every few hours, I really don't have much time for anything else. Trust me, we will find a way to return you to your original *Voyager,* if we can. But for now, we must focus on the problem at hand."

"Captain, if I may," Chakotay-two said.

She nodded at him, not sure what he was going to bring up.

"With your permission," he said, "I would like my away team to continue to act as if they were on an away mission to another ship. We are here as your guests, but also as officers. So please, put us to work, but I wanted to reassure you that none of us expect to have the positions we normally have on our *Voyager.*"

Torres-two clenched a fist and rested it on her knee.

Janeway noted the movement, but didn't acknowledge it. "Thank you, Chakotay-two," she said. "That certainly makes things easier."

She took a deep breath. Now for the part of the

meeting that was the most important. "We're going to need to find a solution to this problem. It is so large as to be overwhelming, but we can't look at each individual death. It will diminish all of us."

She glanced around to make sure everyone was following, then went on. "We need to focus on the larger picture at hand. We need to focus on these poor people as a unit. If we can find a way to stop them from being transported over here, we've accomplished a large victory. We will, of course, save as many as we can, but we cannot, as Tuvok has said, put ourselves at risk. That would be detrimental to everyone."

She made that section of her speech clear, knowing that her own staff had heard a different version before, but realizing that the newcomers needed to hear it.

"It has become clear to me since the away team arrived," she continued, "that we are working with only half the information we need to solve this problem. Chakotay-two, can you fill us in on what happened on the planet? What is causing these poor people to be transported here, and what do you see as a solution?"

Chakotay-two glanced at Torres-two.

"With your permission, Captain," Torres-two said, "I would like to answer that."

Janeway nodded. Torres-two launched into a description of the technology and the problems she had had on R'Lee's planet. When she finished that, she started into a description of the problems she had had with the local population, but stopped after only a few sentences, looking stricken.

She must have realized, at that moment, that the people she had been having difficulties with were now floating in a containment field where the planet had once been. Those people would die in the next few hours if *Voyager* didn't come up with some sort of solution.

"I . . . ah . . . that's all," Torres-two said, and looked down at her hands. Both fists were clenched now, and there was a tension in her shoulders that hadn't been there before. Janeway felt a compassion for her, knowing how difficult this was to deal with.

"Thank you, Torres-two," Janeway said gently.

Torres-two nodded once without looking up.

"So basically," Torres said, "we have a transport system gone bad, with no way to shut it off."

Torres-two looked up. The only real difference between the two women was in their forehead ridges. Torres's stood out slightly more. "Yes," she said. "That's right."

Janeway watched them, saying nothing. Maybe they would be able to work together after all.

"You tried to stop it, I trust," Torres said.

"There is no way to shut it off," Torres-two said. "Once it started, it can't be stopped."

"I don't believe in the word 'can't,'" Torres said, her voice ringing with challenge.

"Neither do I," Torres-two said, "but sometimes facts are facts."

"And sometimes," Janeway said, wishing for that moment of peace she had felt just a second before, "there is more than one way to approach a problem. We've been focusing on the people transporting here. We haven't thought of what causes it, not really. And now we have that information. We need to figure out how to use it."

She turned to Ensign Kim. "Is there a way of knowing if our message got through to the other *Voyager*s?"

"No, Captain," Kim said. "At least not until the next shift. But I don't see why it didn't."

"The next shift," Janeway said. Billions would die while they got their information. She had never felt so helpless before. Every second they delayed was a second that took billions of people closer to death.

Janeway turned to Torres. "Have you found any way of moving the containment field into the next universe while maintaining one here?"

Torres shook her head. "My problem," she said, "is that we don't have the resources, Captain. If I could figure out a way to beam the containment field to the next universe, there would be no way to maintain it."

"And you'd have to build another containment field for each shift," Torres-two said.

Torres nodded. "That's right. The drain on our systems would be exponential."

"Unless you could figure out a way to make the containment field self-sufficient," Torres-two said.

"But for how long?" Torres asked. "It might take us days, even weeks to solve this."

Her words echoed in the ready room. It couldn't take days. It couldn't take weeks. The crew couldn't sustain their fight for that long. Janeway wasn't sure how much death people could see and not go mad.

She quickly checked how much time they had. Just over an hour and a half to the next shift. "Torres-two, I want you to help Torres find a way to move that containment field out of the way of the next shift, and set up a new one for those coming in."

"Captain," Torres said, "the problems—"

"Are for the long term," Janeway said. "We need to explore temporary solutions. We need to buy some time for some of those poor souls. You two will work together on this."

"Aye, Captain," both Torreses said in unison, both in the same reluctant tone.

"Kes-two," Janeway said, "I want you to return to the sickbay with Kes and help there with the survivors in any fashion you can."

The two women nodded in unison. Neelix watched them warily. He made no move to be near either of them.

"Chakotay-two and Paris-two, I want you on the bridge. We're going to need all the help we can get when messages from other *Voyager*s start pouring in during the next shift."

If they start pouring in, Janeway thought. But she

couldn't speak that possibility. She had to believe help would arrive. "I want to be ready by then."

"Understood, Captain," Chakotay-two said.

Chakotay glanced up at his double and nodded, obviously about to say the same thing, but just too tired to get it out as fast.

Janeway couldn't even bring herself to smile. The problem facing them was so huge she had no idea where to even begin, let alone how to solve it.

All she knew was that *Voyager*'s trip home had stopped right here until a solution was found.

If there was one to be found.

CHAPTER
28

Time: The ninetieth shift
Location: 2,544 parallel universes to the right of ours

JANEWAY LEANED BACK IN HER CHAIR, FINGERS clutching the armrests.

Billions dead.

Even more dying.

Her mind couldn't wrap itself around the idea, but her heart could. Entire populations disappearing from their worlds in the space of a heartbeat, only to end up in space with no air, no heat, no way to survive.

How numbingly awful.

She had never heard her briefing room so quiet.

She swiveled her chair. Chakotay sat beside her as he often did, but it was not the Chakotay she knew. This Chakotay had come from a different *Voyager,* and if she looked at him casually, she wouldn't be able to tell any difference. He seemed like her Chakotay. He even reacted to the news the same way. He said nothing, but his skin had become ashen.

The new Kes sat across from Neelix. He had stared at her through much of the meeting, apparently trying to see the difference, but no longer. He was staring at the empty viewscreen where Janeway's counterpart a hundred and some universes over—a bloodied, battered, haunted woman—had managed to relay a message across space and thousands of universes.

Paris was staring at his hands, and Torres had a fierce expression on her face: fierce and frightened.

Tuvok was frowning as if he were doing calculations in his head. Ensign Kim was working the console in front of him, doing the calculations Janeway had asked for so that she could see for herself the devastation that the other Janeway had described.

Whether she saw it or not, though, she knew it existed. She knew herself well enough—she knew that no matter how she wore her hair, no matter how tiny the physical differences were, she would do everything she could, give all she had to save even a fraction of the billions who were dying before her.

Even if it killed her.

She had to speak. She knew no one on her senior staff would unless she did so first.

"Well," she said, "now we know what happened to the inhabitants of this world."

Neelix sank into his seat. "I'm not sure it's something I wanted to know."

"Me, either," Paris said. He looked at Janeway. His green eyes were bloodshot. "That world below showed me a pretty contented people. It seemed almost idyllic, Captain."

"Every place looks idyllic without people," Torres said.

"All I meant is," Paris continued, a little softer, as if his opinion wasn't as valuable after she had spoken, "that we need to do something, if we can."

Chakotay opened his mouth, probably to say something about all peoples being worth saving, no matter who they were. To forestall him, Janeway said, "I agree. We do need to take action."

"We need to consider carefully the ramifications of what we have heard," Tuvok said. "The population of the planet below, the vanished people who so seemed to have intrigued Mr. Paris have shifted ninety universes from this one."

"And since the populations of the planets upstream," Neelix said, "are being killed in empty space, there is no one to shift in here." His words were soft, perhaps to ameliorate the distress of Paris.

"Exactly," Janeway said.

"I can't imagine how that *Voyager* crew is coping with all the death," Kes said.

Janeway could. It would be a frantic, desperate effort to save the living and create a place in which those being deposited into space would be able to survive. *Voyager* wouldn't be able to hold even a tiny fraction of them all. And any containment field would be limited by *Voyager*'s meager energy reserves.

She would be doing what she could, all the while

knowing it was not—and would never be—enough.

She leaned forward, her stomach twisting at the very thought of facing such horrors.

"Well," she said, "since there are over a hundred destroyed planets between us and that *Voyager,* we are one of those ships that Captain Janeway asked for help. I know we have just seen the message. I know this is new to us, but I also know that time is of the essence here. Does anyone have any ideas on what we can do to stop this?"

The silence filled the room like a heavy weight, pounding down on all of them. Torres frowned. Tuvok templed his fingers and tapped them against his mouth. Harry Kim did not look up from his console. The beeps from his work were the only sound in the room.

Janeway took a breath. She didn't have any ideas either.

Not yet.

But once she studied the implications, she would.

She knew it.

"All right then," she said. "We have exactly one and a half hours until the next shift. We will meet back here in an hour. At that time, we will have solutions. Several solutions. Is that clear?"

Her senior staff nodded, none of them meeting her gaze. She could feel their emotions without even being told. They didn't believe there was a solution.

She stood. "Every problem can be resolved. No matter how vast the problem is."

"Yes, Captain," Chakotay said. "But at what cost?"

"Cost is for the historians to decide, Chakotay," Janeway said. "We will do the best we can. We will save as many lives as we can. Entire planets are depending on us. The least we can do is offer up ideas."

Harry Kim pushed his chair back. "And the best we can do is help them," he said.

"All of them," Paris added.

Janeway nodded. She watched her staff file out. Then she turned to a screen and pulled up the records of the last shift. Every sensor had been focused on that event. Somewhere in all that information she knew the answer existed.

She was going to find it.

CHAPTER 29

Time: The ninetieth shift
Location: 2,410 parallel universes to the right
of ours

ENGINEERING WAS HOT, AND SMELLED FAINTLY OF
decaying flesh and blood, even though there were
no patients here. In this area, as well as the bridge
and the captain's ready room, no patients crowded
the halls. Everything looked normal, except for the
blood-spattered ensigns running through on occasion, looking for a spanner or something that
would help them convert another storage compartment into a sickbay.

The next thing they'd do was convert Jeffries
tubes.

Torres hunched over the engineering console.
Her station. Her counterpart, Torres-two (what a
stupid name. Why couldn't she be called something else? She needed a completely different
name—Klingon, of course—but one that established her as the other, as not-Torres) had tried to
use that console, but Torres had reminded Torres-
two (the name definitely had to go!) that she was

part of an away team, on the ship as a guest, not as a staff member.

Torres-two had growled at her, but she had moved.

Torres hated having her here. The woman was arrogant and stubborn. Her brow ridges were too sharp and so were her eyes. She seemed to think that she knew everything, and that wasn't possible. She came from a different universe, and everything about her was wrong.

Except the way her hands flew over her console. She clearly did have engineering skills.

And why wouldn't she? She had the same training as Torres.

Torres shook her head sharply. All this endless speculation was about the wrong thing. Who would have thought that she would be distracted by this impostor? This woman she mostly hated and secretly admired? Who would have thought?

"If you keep staring at me," Torres-two said, "you won't get anything done."

"The only way you knew that I was even looking at you is because you're the one who was staring," Torres said.

They glared at each other. It was like looking in a mirror, a mirror that distorted. Whenever Torres-two moved her face, it did not match the expression on Torres's face.

A mirror with a mind of its own.

They growled again, softly, then turned their attention to their consoles.

At the same time.

Torres forced herself to think of the problem at hand. She could smell it, since the processors weren't handling the air properly. Life support was overextended.

The resources of the ship were already at capacity, and the captain wanted them to create yet another containment field? It wasn't possible. None of this was possible.

And even if they did create another containment field, in two hours, they would have to create a third. And then a fourth, and on and on until *Voyager* herself became a floating hulk, without the energy reserves to power the ship, let alone life support.

The captain would kill them all trying to save a fraction of the billions pouring into this universe.

And the ironic thing was that Torres couldn't blame her.

She couldn't blame her at all.

Torres-two glanced from the panel in front of her to Torres. "The ship is dangerously low on all resources."

Torres started. Had the other woman just had the same train of thought Torres had? How eerie. Especially when one was raised to think of oneself as a unique being.

Torres swallowed. "I know," she said, trying not to let Torres-two notice how unnerved she was. "Even if we figure out a way to move the first containment field, I doubt we'll have enough oxygen and power to create another."

"I agree," Torres-two said. Her fingers still

worked the console as she spoke. Apparently her mind was as capable as Torres's when it came to doing two things at once.

"Maybe we're going about this wrong," Torres--two said.

"How could we be going about this wrong?" Torres snapped. "There can't be a right way. No one has ever done this before. No one has ever attempted it—"

"I wasn't criticizing you," her counterpart snapped equally as fiercely. Torres recognized the tone: It was her *Don't be stupid when I'm trying to get something done here* voice. "I simply think there might be a more efficient method, one that doesn't strain the ship's energy reserves quite as seriously."

Torres put a hand to her face. Her skin was hot and sticky with sweat. She was exhausted. She had been on her feet, thinking on her feet, for hours, faced with impossible numbers of dying human-oids, and knowing the task before her was hopeless. This new Torres, Torres-two, hadn't had those experiences.

Her mind was clearer, even though Torres hated to admit that.

"All right then," Torres said. "What's your brilliant idea?"

Torres-two ignored the sarcasm. "From what I can gather, there are at least a couple million living beings in that containment field."

"So?" Torres said, wishing her counterpart would get to the point.

But Torres-two wasn't speaking to her. Apparently Torres-two's mind was already several light-years ahead of the conversation. Torres knew how that worked. She had done it herself every day, infuriating her ensigns.

Torres-two was hunched over the engineering control panel, one hand pressed on her mouth and the other doing calculations. Rather than quiz her, Torres came up beside her and peered at the console.

Torres-two's fingers were dancing over the control panel. So that was what people saw when she was working at top speed. No wonder they stayed out of her way.

Then Torres saw what her double was working on. "What good will the transporter do?" she said. "There's nowhere to transport these people. There's no planet close and no more room on the ship."

"There's plenty of room on the ship," Torres-two said, pointing at the panel. "If we leave them in the buffer."

For an instant Torres's tired mind wanted to just give up, say it wasn't possible, but then the fog of tiredness lifted and the challenge of making Torres-two's idea work took over. "We would have to adjust the transporter beams for wide scan—"

"—and convert the holodeck computers into buffers," Torres-two said, finishing the other's sentence.

"We could also use the shuttles' computers and buffers," Torres said.

"That way we don't have to move or create a new containment field," Torres-two said.

They paused at the same time, took a breath together, and stared at each other. Torres felt stronger for a moment, as if her own mental capacity hadn't doubled, but quadrupled. She resisted the urge to grin and said instead, "Something like this has never been tried before."

"There's never been a situation like this before," Torres-two said.

"That's for sure," Torres said.

They looked at each other, one tired, one energized and excited. Then they both nodded before turning back to work. One Torres could make wonders of engineering happen. Two would create miracles.

CHAPTER
30

Time: The ninetieth shift
Location: Our universe

THE BRIDGE WAS SILENT, EXCEPT FOR THE NORMAL BIPS and beeps of the equipment. Janeway sat in her command chair, her science console up. She was working.

Her entire crew was working, from Chakotay to Tuvok, on finding a solution. Some worked in isolation, as did the folks on the bridge, while others were working in groups, as did many of the ensigns on the other decks.

The members of the former away team who were on the bridge, Paris, Chakotay, and Torres, seemed to be working harder than the others. Perhaps to prove that they were as worthy of being there as the trio that really belonged in this universe. Perhaps to keep their minds off the fact that they were two universes away from their ship, away from the place that had become their home.

Janeway checked the time remaining until the next shift for the sixth time in the last half hour.

Thirty-five minutes. She forced herself to go back to poring over the data on her screen. In all her years, she hadn't felt this helpless and out of control. She knew that in thousands of other universes other Janeways and *Voyager* crews were furiously working to find a solution to this problem. She understood the restriction the one captain had put on the others for responses. Having thousands of messages come in, all in a three-second span, would be overwhelming. Besides, what twenty or so *Voyager* crews might figure out as a solution would, more than likely, be the same as what a thousand crews would come up with.

So she agreed with the other captain's decision on limiting the number of crews sending ideas, but that agreement didn't help. She was used to taking action, not waiting for someone else to take it. That's why she had the crew working at full speed to come up with answers of their own. Inside she felt *her* crew could come up with the best idea.

And she had no doubt that thousands of Janeways just like her were having their crews do the same, for the exact same reason.

Paris cursed softly and balanced a fist on the edge of his console. He wasn't a scientist. He was one of the best pilots she had ever known. Janeway was having him look at various piloting options: What would happen if he flew *Voyager* into the opening between universes that the pulse created? What would be the optimal speed to do so? Was it even possible?

She wasn't sure Paris could do the necessary

calculations and come up with the correct answer. He would be working on supposition like the rest of them.

He looked so much like the Paris she knew. He acted like that man. And yet, that single curl falling across his forehead was like a brand, screaming that he was not the same man at all.

Different or not, stranger or not, she knew the essence of him. And she knew she could trust him. Just as she could trust Torres, Chakotay, and Kes. They were not the same crew, but they did fill the gaps left by the other away team—and conveniently, they had the same skills.

Janeway smiled to herself. Strange the things the mind did when it was overwhelmed. She focused on her screen for another moment, frowning.

They were missing something. Another small detail. Something so small as to be nearly invisible. But like every other small detail on this day, the detail was the crucial piece of information, the thing that would solve the larger puzzle.

If only she could see it.

Or maybe she wasn't supposed to see it. Maybe she needed to feel it, as she first felt that subspace pulse, so long ago in her ready room. That shudder through the ship, so different from the norm, and yet so slight as to be unnoticed by all but those most attuned to *Voyager*.

She wasn't attuned to this area of space. She had never been here before. She had never seen the Birsibans before. She didn't know when that subtle difference occurred.

If only she could determine it. Contacting R'Lee wouldn't help. His race wasn't technologically advanced enough. They hadn't even understood the problem they caused.

No. It was something she would have to figure out, and quickly.

Thirty-two minutes until the next shift. Time. Sometimes it moved so slowly. Sometimes so quickly. And never, it seemed, in control.

CHAPTER 31

Time: The ninetieth shift
Location: 2,544 parallel universes to the right of ours

JANEWAY SAT IN HER CHAIR IN THE BRIEFING ROOM. She had faced numerous decisions over her years of command, but most had been cut and dried. Most had been choices that she could see.

She had spent the last hour trying to find a solution to this problem, trying to find a choice— any choice—in this matter, and coming up with nothing.

That wasn't exactly true. She hadn't come up with nothing. She had come with maybe a dozen ideas, and had checked them through the computer. Some she hadn't had to check. Others she had.

The results were all the same. None of the solutions worked.

She leaned back in her chair. Everyone had arrived but Torres. Janeway didn't have the time to wait. Torres was usually reliable, but this was not her Torres. Perhaps the other Janeway hadn't tamed Torres, hadn't shown her how she could function well in a normal crew.

Then the double doors swished open and Torres hurried in. "Sorry," she said, just as the Torres from this *Voyager* would have said. "I was running a calculation. It took a moment longer than I planned."

"We don't have a moment, Lieutenant," Tuvok said.

"I know," Torres said, bowing her head. "I'm sorry."

There wasn't time for recriminations. There wasn't time for anything. Janeway glanced at her senior staff. They were all in their seats, all with identical expressions.

They hadn't found anything either.

But she would let them tell her that.

"All right, people," Janeway said. "We have twenty-eight minutes until the next shift. What have you come up with?"

As she expected, no one said a word. She sighed and threaded her fingers together. She hadn't come up with anything either. She still wasn't exactly sure what was causing the shifting of the population from universe to universe, let alone how to stop it.

"I said earlier that no problem was too great for us." She leaned forward. "I meant it. We couldn't find the solution individually. Perhaps we can do so together. I had chosen not to do this initially because sometimes this procedure takes too much time. But now it's all we have left. If we're going to brainstorm, people—and we are—keep it short and to the point."

Around her everyone nodded.

"Let's trace this back to the beginning," Janeway said, "and see if there is something we missed."

She looked at Tuvok, knowing he would help her begin the discussion. He wasn't subject to the disappointment and despair that seemed to have taken over the crew since the other Janeway's message.

He nodded at her, then said, "This phenomenon began when the Birsibans initiated a worldwide transportation service."

"Somehow," Torres said, caught up in the moment just as the Torres who belonged to this *Voyager* would have been, "and for some reason we haven't figured out, the power surge and the worldwide transporter units ripped a hole in the walls between the universes. Possibly they started the system right over the top of a space-time anomaly."

"Or created one when they started the machinery," Janeway said. There was something about what they were talking about that was eating at Janeway. A feeling that the solution was right there, if only she could just see it, haunted her.

She frowned, but kept the discussion going, making a mental note to remember the feeling, to let the thought, buried in her subconscious, rise to the surface.

Torres was shaking her head. "It doesn't matter how the event started. What's important is stopping it. But I doubt that even destroying every transportation center on every planet in all the universes would stop it now. From what I could tell down below, this has gone far, far beyond that simple system of theirs."

"So why the trigger every time their power comes up and discharges?" Paris asked. His hair was tousled, as if he'd been running his fingers through it. "Couldn't we just destroy their power sources?"

"I have been asking myself that same question," Torres said. "But the power from the Birsiban underground storage is only a very, *very* small fraction of the total power being used by this event. I would imagine at the beginning it was that small amount of power that triggered the bigger surge, but now that surge is on a continuing cycle."

"One we can't stop," Chakotay said.

"Exactly," Janeway said. She found it interesting that the people most involved in this debate were the away team from the other ship. Her own senior staff members were watching, as if they hadn't even had this many ideas.

Of course, the situation, while extremely important to them, was still abstract. For the new Paris, Chakotay, Kes, and Torres, this situation was very, very personal.

"So even if every *Voyager* destroyed a power source," Paris asked, "it wouldn't be enough?"

Torres shook her head tiredly. "I doubt it. And remember, there are only *Voyager*s on every other planet."

"Besides," Janeway said, feeling this line of thinking had gone far enough, "the extra energy coming from our destroying the power sources might trigger a quicker event cycle, or a chain reaction that would destroy all the planets in all the universes: an outcome much, much worse."

Her comments stopped the room cold.

Tuvok raised his chin slightly, as if the very thought had rocked him.

Harry Kim was shaking his head.

"Mr. Kim?" Janeway said, seeing something in his eyes, something that she couldn't quite define.

"I don't know, Captain," Kim said. "All I keep thinking about is that the only way to stop this was to never have it start in the first place."

Janeway felt a shiver run down her back. What had been bothering her had finally fallen into place. Mr. Kim was completely correct.

This had to be stopped before it started.

Torres was also looking at Kim with that faraway, thinking look. She had picked up on the same thing.

"Torres," Janeway said, "can it be done?"

Torres thought for a moment more, then looked at Janeway. "I know we can make it back in time—"

"I thought you told me, when we went back to Old Earth, that time travel was not a recommended procedure," Neelix said to Janeway.

She nodded at him. "It is something we shy away from."

"There are rules and regulations," Tuvok said, "as well as grave dangers involved in time travel. We are trained not to think of it as an option."

"Except in extreme circumstances," Paris said.

"Which this is," Janeway said. She turned to Torres. "I want to hear your reservations."

Torres frowned. "I don't know if we'd survive the paradoxes involved. Or even be able to stop the event in these universes. We might only create a new set of universes in which the event never happens, while leaving these to continue."

"Paradoxes?" Neelix asked, looking confused.

Torres nodded. "If we went back to a time right ahead of the first shift, there would be two *Voyager*s existing in the same place at the same time. This *Voyager* with"—she glanced at the other members of the away team—"me, and Tom, Chakotay, and Kes, and this *Voyager* as it was several hours ago, with its own Torres, Paris, Chakotay, and Kes light-years from here."

"At that point in time that *Voyager* would never answer the distress call," Paris said.

"While this *Voyager* would be trying to fix a problem that hasn't even started yet," Torres said.

"So?" Neelix asked. "I thought we would want that."

Janeway sighed. She hated time paradoxes, and she hated explaining them. But it had to be discussed. "It could create its own share of problems, Mr. Neelix. Problems akin to the ones we're facing, the ones we're already experiencing with the wrong away team aboard our ship."

the ones we're already experiencing with the wrong away team aboard our ship."

Torres nodded, even though she was a member of that incorrect away team. "There are several problems. Imagine, if you will, that we stop the event. The paradox is immense. If we stop the event, then there would be no subspace waves and distress call to summon us to the planet, thus we could have never gone back in time to fix it."

"In other words," Paris said, "this timeline ends. This ship and all we've gone through would cease to exist, right back to the moment we felt the first shift?"

"That's right," Torres said. "Because we would already exist before we got the distress call, or felt that first shift. And we would never feel it."

"I'm getting a headache," Neelix said.

"It's all very logical," Tuvok said.

Janeway stared into the silence that filled the room as each of them thought about suddenly ceasing to exist. Was this how the other Janeway felt when she sacrificed that other *Voyager* for this *Voyager*? They would, in essence, be doing the same thing all over again. Only this time she would be the one sacrificing the ship.

"Captain," Chakotay said, "I'm more concerned with the first worry that Torres had. What if we simply split off a new set of universes, one set of universes where we fixed the problem by going back in time, leaving another set of universes and the billions and billions here, in these universes, to die?"

Torres nodded. "It is possible."

"But not likely," Janeway said. "We would be remaining on this one event track. This event is linked to all the *Voyager*s. If we stop it, the timeline ends."

Torres nodded in slow agreement. "It just might work. If enough *Voyager*s stopped the first initial startup, then the power being drawn from all the systems wouldn't occur."

"And if we ceased to exist," Paris said, "how would we know if we succeeded?"

"We wouldn't," Torres said.

"But we would know if we failed," Janeway said.

CHAPTER 32

Time: The ninetieth shift
Location: 2,410 parallel universes to the right
of ours

"TWELVE MINUTES UNTIL THE NEXT SHIFT," ENSIGN Kim said. The bridge was quiet, even though it was fully staffed. The faint odor of blood and injured bodies floated in the recycled air. The life support system was overloaded, and even though none of the patients beamed aboard were on the bridge, their presence was here, in the scent, in the growing heat, in the underlying stress.

Chakotay shook his shoulders to loosen them. He had never felt such tension. Every muscle in his body was tight. He glanced at Chakotay-two, bent over an auxiliary work station. Chakotay-two's fingers on his left hand were working through an old relaxation charm, one Chakotay—they—had learned as a boy.

Chakotay shuddered. He didn't like to have his movements mirrored, his thoughts mirrored, his behaviors mirrored. He had thought he was unique, only to discover an infinite number of himself existing in an infinite number of universes. Yes, they all had small differences, but the small differences were hardly counted.

They hardly counted at all.

"Is the message ready for the away team's home ship?" Janeway asked. She was sitting in the command chair. Chakotay was working at his station on the upper level of the bridge. He hadn't been able to sit in his place beside her. He found that he had to be busy, that he needed something else to think about.

"Yes, Captain," Kim said.

Chakotay knew that the message was a brief one intended for only the *Voyager* two universes away, letting that captain know that her away team was safe. Chakotay-two had thanked the captain when she suggested they send it, but a shadow had crossed his face. Chakotay had understood it. He felt it too.

They were sending messages on the backs of the dead.

The thought was the one he'd been trying to suppress. He clenched his fists, just as Janeway turned to him. She noted the movement, then glanced at Chakotay-two, then back at him. Her eyes were compassionate, but her expression was firm. It said, *Keep hold of yourself, Chakotay. I need you.*

They all needed each other, if they were going to find a solution to this.

"Are Torres and Torres-two ready?" Janeway asked.

Chakotay glanced down at his board. The two chief engineers were very close to clearing out the live humanoids in the containment field. Those humanoids patterns were compacted down, then stored in every extra computer storage space the ship had. It was a solution that would last for exactly one shift. After that they would have to come up with another idea to save the millions shifting into the containment field.

"They are," Chakotay said. It would save almost a million lives. But only until the next shift, which was minutes away. Then they had two and a half hours to come up with a permanent solution, or another temporary one.

He hoped for the permanent one.

Captain Janeway nodded, the exhaustion clear on her face. "Good."

"Are we ready to receive any message sent to us?"

Chakotay-two moved over and stood beside Ensign Kim. "We are, Captain."

"And my recorded message is ready to send?"

Chakotay had never heard the Captain be so methodical before. But with the crew this tired, it was better that she was checking every detail.

"Everything's ready, Captain," Chakotay said.

Janeway just nodded and sat down in her chair. "Then I guess there's nothing to do but wait."

"Six minutes until the next shift," Ensign Kim said.

Six minutes until they needed another solution.

Chakotay hoped the messages carried on the backs of the dead would work.

He hoped the other *Voyager*s had come up with a solution.

Because this *Voyager* was rapidly running out of options.

CHAPTER
33

Time: The ninety-first shift
Location: Our universe

AND SO IT BEGAN.

The light hit, and the universes opened up around her, planets ringing the one below, mirror images laid on top of each other, and around every other one, a *Voyager*.

Two universes to her left (using her counterpart, the beleaguered Janeway's, description of the phenomenon) was the *Voyager* her current away team had come from. The three that were on the bridge, Chakotay, Torres, and Paris, were watching it, as if they could see where they had come from.

The rest of the crew was doing what Janeway wanted them to do: They were looking to the right, hoping to see the emptiness two thousand universes away, the emptiness into which all the populations of all the planets would eventually pour.

And die.

Janeway allowed her gaze to move down the line

to the right, staring for the break in the long string of planets. She really couldn't see it, since it was over two thousand universes away. But she had seen the pictures sent by that other Captain Janeway on the last shift, and that was enough to make it all clear.

Too clear.

She no longer looked on the shift as something beautiful or fascinating, not now that she knew billions were dying, and billions more would die.

There was nothing pretty about that.

"Captain," Ensign Kim said, "we have messages coming in."

Janeway turned away from the screen, and felt a relief she wasn't sure she liked as she did so.

"Subspace impact—" Tuvok said "—Now!"

The ship shuddered slightly, then calmed. The universes vanished off the screen. Janeway found she was gripping the arms of her command chair.

She took a deep breath. "How many messages, Mr. Kim?"

"Twenty-seven, Captain," he said. "We've received another one from the *Voyager* that sent the first message, and twenty-six from other *Voyager*s."

She could foresee a major communication breakdown if she didn't forestall it immediately. But she wasn't quite sure how yet. She would let her mind work on it while she continued gathering information. "Were any of the messages directed at us?"

Kim shook his head. "We only picked them up, Captain."

"As, I'm sure, did the other *Voyager*s," Tuvok said.

Janeway nodded. "And the other twenty-six messages? Where did they originate?"

Kim opened his mouth and then closed it. He shrugged. The communication difficulty had hit. "The twenty-six messages are from the *Voyager*s in either direction of original message sender."

"This gets confusing," Paris said.

"That it does, Mr. Paris," Janeway said. She had to figure out a way to distinguish between the *Voyager*s. "Mr. Kim, how many universes away from us is that original message sender?"

He frowned as he looked at his console. "It's two thousand, four hundred and ten universes from here," he said, sounding a bit astonished at the number. He had mentioned it earlier, when the first message arrived, but apparently the number hadn't really sunken in.

"That's a lot of universes," Paris said.

"Not when measured in two-and-a-half hour intervals," Torres said softly.

Janeway knew what she meant. It wouldn't take that long for the original population of the planet below them to hit that emptiness, that ghost planet of bodies, in space.

"All right," Janeway said. "We call that one *Voyager twenty-four-ten*. Mr. Kim, label each of the incoming messages with the same type of number, depending on their distance of origin from us."

"Aye, Captain," Kim said.

"How soon until we can view the message from *Voyager twenty-four-ten?*"

"It's almost ready, Captain," Kim said. "It was not as compressed as the first one."

Janeway stood. She wasn't sure how she would face this. She didn't like seeing herself this way, nor did she like being two thousand four hundred and ten universes away from a disaster. She wanted to be in the middle of it.

And she wanted to be as far away from it as she could.

"It's ready," Kim said.

"Put it on screen, Mr. Kim."

He nodded.

Janeway watched as a different version of herself filled the screen. This was the version who was in the middle of the disaster—and who was clearly running out of options.

Her strange orange and black uniform was rumpled, and more hair had fallen from the braided corona around her face. Lines had formed on the side of her mouth, lines that this Janeway wondered would ever disappear. Her eyes were small dots of pain in the center of her face.

"The first part of this message," the Janeway on screen said, "is directed to the *Voyager* two universes to our left. Your away team is safe on board."

Behind Janeway on the bridge, Torres gasped. Janeway felt a shiver run down her back. She hadn't realized—she hadn't thought of—the away teams her counterparts had sent, and how one would have ended up in that nightmare of dead and dying bodies forming in the asteroid belt.

The Janeway on screen continued, "They were not injured in the shift into space. They were lucky enough to shift into a containment area we have set up to rescue as many as we can."

"Lucky," Chakotay repeated. He sounded stunned.

"It's better than landing in the vacuum of space with no way to breathe," Paris said and shuddered.

Janeway ignored the chatter. She was shocked at the idea of an away team getting caught in this mess. The members of another ship's away team, already two universes away from their own, had to be even more stunned.

"To the rest of the *Voyager*s," the other Janeway was saying, "remain in position if you would. My team will analyze any ideas sent to us this shift and will send out a plan on the next shift."

She brought a hand to her ruined braid. The hand was shaking, belying the calmness in her voice. "I understand," she said softly, "that many more will die before we can act. But I see no other choice. I am sorry."

She nodded her head once, as if she couldn't contain the emotion inside. "Janeway out."

Her image disappeared, replaced by the planet below. The planet in this universe. It was beautiful, with its blues and greens and swirling clouds.

Beautiful.

And, at the moment, deadly.

Two and a half hours.

Two and a half hours to come up with another solution. And even then, it would be too late to save those lives.

The lives being lost were so many that they were still abstractions to this Janeway.

Her counterpart, two thousand four hundred and ten universes away, was seeing each of those lives as reality.

A horrible reality.

Janeway turned to Kim. He was staring at the screen. So were the other members of the bridge crew.

She had to snap them into action. "How long until the other messages can be ready?"

Kim looked at her, flushed, then looked down at his console. "I'll have the first for you in a few minutes, Captain," he said.

Janeway touched her own hair, realized it was a nervous gesture she shared with Janeways all the way down the universe chain, and remembered the shaking hand of her counterpart. The shaking hand and ruined hairstyle.

How different they were at the moment.

Janeway's hair, here, on this ship, was neat as a pin. And the very thought, oddly, made her feel guilty, made her feel as if she weren't working hard enough.

Maybe she wasn't.

She glanced at the screen once more, then took a

deep breath. "I want to see the senior officers in the briefing room in thirty minutes. That includes members of the away team."

"Aye, Captain," Chakotay said.

"Mr. Kim," Janeway said, "I want those messages relayed to my ready room as soon as possible. The rest of you keep searching for answers. I want something, anything, in the next thirty minutes. People are dying. We do not have the luxury of waiting for an answer to strike us. We must search it out. Am I making myself clear?"

"Perfectly, Captain," Paris said.

She glanced at him. He was staring at the screen. He had spoken without sarcasm.

"Very good," she said, and headed to her ready room.

She would look the messages over first, before she met with the crew, just to be prepared. She had an idea what the other *Voyager*s were going to propose. She knew what she would have proposed. She wanted to have a little time to think it over, alone.

CHAPTER
34

Time: The ninety-first shift
Location: 2,410 parallel universes to the right
of ours

JANEWAY SAT IN HER CHAIR, PRESSED AGAINST THE
wall of her ready room. The small screen on her
desk played out the last of the messages.

The room was packed with her crew, and the
four additional members from the *Voyager* two
universes over. The ready room had grown hot; the
life support system was becoming more and more
overloaded. The additional bodies on the ship, plus
the use of the computer's buffers for storage of even
more humanoids, was taxing every level of the
ship.

Janeway wanted to believe that the growing smell
came from the overtaxed life support systems, but
she suspected it also came from her crew. They'd
had no time to clean up, and they were operating in
heat, sweating and worrying and doing the best
they could against overwhelming odds.

Absolutely overwhelming odds.

The other Janeways, the other *Voyager*s, seemed

to understand that. They had come up with solutions as she had asked, and they had surprised her. Janeway hadn't imagined that all the suggestions from all the *Voyager*s would come down to the same thing: They had to stop this before it started.

As the image of the last Janeway faded from the screen, this Janeway, braid nearly pulled free, orange and black uniform clinging to her, cleared her throat. The crew turned to her as one unit.

"Well," she said, her voice rasping with exhaustion, "I want to hear your reactions."

For a moment, no one spoke. Then Paris-two, who was sitting across the room from his counterpart, dipped his head slightly.

"Mr. Paris?" she said, then added, "two" before the other Paris could speak.

He shrugged. "I was just thinking." He scratched his head, glanced at Paris, then glanced away. "If we return in time to a point before the shifts started, and stop them, won't this ship and crew cease to exist?"

"From what we know of time travel," Janeway said, "that is exactly what will happen."

"Cease to exist?" Neelix said. His voice was pitched oddly as if he could barely get the words out. He was sitting across the room from both Keses, as if facing two of them was more than he could bear.

"I am afraid so, Mr. Neelix," Tuvok said. "The theory works thus: If we succeed in our mission when we travel back in time, and stop the events that brought us to this position we are in now, this timeline would cease to exist. And we would cease to exist also, right along with it."

Janeway clasped her hands together. She would sacrifice her ship, just as the other Janeway had in that plasma cloud so long ago. How ironic.

How appropriate.

"Will we save all the people that have died?" Neelix said.

"Yes," Janeway said.

Neelix looked at the others, his crest of hair bobbing as he did so. "Then I vote we go back."

Janeway laughed. The sound was tired, raspy, and a bit surprised. She didn't know she had a laugh left in her. "This isn't a vote, Mr. Neelix. But I do thank you for your input. Anyone else?"

Both Torres and Torres-two started to speak at the same moment. Then they stopped, glanced at each other, and frowned.

At least, Janeway thought, it wasn't a glare.

Then Torres-two nodded at Torres to continue. Tuvok raised an eyebrow as he met Janeway's gaze. She shrugged almost imperceptibly. Both Torreses were working together. That was a good sign.

"Captain," Torres said, "the problem I have is that the other *Voyager*s assumed that stopping the initial surge of energy on half the planets would stop the entire event."

Janeway felt her stomach twist ever so slightly. They *had* made that assumption. "So, Lieutenant, with *Voyager*s missing on half the universes, you believe that stopping the initial surge on the others wouldn't be enough?"

Torres scratched the back of her neck, tilting her head as she did so. She glanced at Torres-two, who was frowning in just the same way.

"That's the problem," Torres said. "I just don't *know.*"

"And if it's not," Chakotay said, "are we any worse off?"

This time Torres-two got in the answer before Torres. "Traveling back in time is not an easy task. And not an exact one."

"We risk destruction," Torres said, "or ending up millions of years off, or worse yet, meeting ourselves and causing some sort of time paradox, the repercussions of which we would have no way of knowing."

"But saving those billions of lives is worth the risk," Chakotay said.

"I'm not saying it isn't," Torres said. "I just want to be sure going back in time is the best solution."

"Right now, it's the only solution," Janeway said. She felt more exhausted than she had felt in her life. "Unless we come up with something else in a very short period of time, we will travel back and see if we can stop this event. Even if it happens in half the universes, that will stop the pile of bodies here."

"Provided," Torres said, "that the system shuts off on half the systems."

"You think it might continue even with half of them not working?" Paris asked.

"The energy buildup is so big," Torres said, "that

I'm not sure what will happen. I don't know, as I've said, if the system is the key to shutting this thing down."

"We wouldn't be shutting it down," Chakotay-two said. "We'd make sure it never starts."

"On half the planets," Torres-two said. "On the other half, it would start."

"And that might be enough," Torres said, "to initiate the effect on all the planets, in all the universes."

"But the captain is right," Neelix said. "It's our only solution."

"It doesn't have to be," Torres-two said. "We could come up with something else."

"We haven't so far," Paris said.

Janeway pushed a strand of hair out of her face. "All right, people," she said, knowing they were wasting time in the discussion. She had to get them moving. "We've got just under two hours to put together a plan to send to the other *Voyager*s."

"Captain," Torres said, sounding tentative, as if she knew she was the one always bringing the bad news. "What are we going to do about those in the containment field?"

Janeway glanced at her. She had known this was going to be a problem, but she had put it out of her mind during the shift. She had hoped for a greater solution—an easier solution—from her sister ships. "Is there any more room in the buffers?"

"No," Torres said.

"Then we let them stay right were they are,"

Janeway said. She swallowed. "I want you working on how to save the billions at this point, not those in the containment field."

Those words seemed to hang cold and hard in the conference room. Janeway couldn't even believe she had just said them. She was thinking things, saying things, that she wouldn't have thought possible two days before. She had done so on the message she had sent the other *Voyager*s, and she had just done so now. She had never been in a situation where her only options seemed to be bad and awful.

"Let's get to work, people," she said. "We don't have much time."

"And neither do those people out there," Torres said, but everyone ignored her.

CHAPTER
35

Time: The ninety-first shift
Location: 2,544 parallel universes to the right
of ours

TORRES HUNCHED OVER HER STATION IN ENGINEERING,
focusing on the numbers in front of her. Around
her everyone worked, silently, alone in their own
thoughts.

Every once in a while she surfaced, realized she
was on the wrong ship, and shuddered, just a little.
She couldn't quite bury the thought. Even the
engineering station, which was right to the exact
detail, seemed wrong. And that was because the
shape of the lip of her console was slightly concave,
in places where she expected it to be convex. She
would hit the difference and it would break her
concentration.

She couldn't afford to have her concentration
broken. Too many lives were at stake.

She glanced around the area. Lieutenant Carey
was focused on his station, and so were some of the
others under his command. They were running the

same figures she was. Only, she suspected, they were getting nowhere.

But she wasn't. She had a feeling she was onto something. Something different.

She leaned back over the console and forced herself to focus.

For what seemed like the hundredth time, she reran the numbers, watching the events of those three seconds of shift from every way she could. Something wasn't right about all this. She knew it. She just had to find out what it was.

Even with all the other *Voyager*s agreeing on the idea of going back in time to fix the problem, she still wasn't convinced it would work. Those missing *Voyager*s meant that every other planet would still start their transport device. And that might be enough to initiate the shifts.

Yet she did agree with one part of the idea: stopping these shifts *before* they started. There didn't seem to be any better solution than that, especially considering how many billions of lives that solution would save.

"But maybe there's a better way to stop it before it starts," she muttered to herself.

She heard the words come out of her mouth and realized that was what she was missing: the key to everything. The most obvious part of the entire mess, the thing that no one was discussing. A better way to go back in time.

Her fingers flew over the board in front of her. After five minutes of quick work, looking at the problem from an entirely different angle, she knew she had it.

Her heart was pounding and her mouth was dry. She had to move quickly.

She punched the comm link. "Captain?"

"Yes, Lieutenant," Janeway said, her voice distant and very distracted.

"I think I may have a better idea."

"In which area?"

"I can't explain it," Torres said. "I need to show you."

"I'm on my way," Janeway said, her voice suddenly sounding more focused and clear.

Torres stood at her board and replayed the image of the shift. The planets moved off in both directions.

Both directions.

It was that very fact that was the key.

It had been staring her right in the face all the time and she hadn't known it. Those two lines of planets had to intersect somewhere. And that intersecting, that *point*, was the same no matter what universe she was in.

That point was right under them.

Under every *Voyager*.

It was that one point that held the answer to stopping this.

She had an idea how to do it now. But no matter how many times she ran the calculations, she couldn't come up with an answer to the one most important question: Would thousands and thousands of *Voyager*s be enough?

CHAPTER
36

Time: The ninety-first shift
Location: 2,410 parallel universes to the right of ours

THE TRIP TO ENGINEERING WAS NOT ONE JANEWAY would soon forget. In the protection of the bridge and her ready room, she hadn't seen all the Birsibans that had been beamed onto the ship. Oh, she had initially, but not after the ship became stuffed with the injured. As she hurried down the corridors, she had had to step over the limbs of people who weren't hurt badly enough for the Doctor to treat yet. He, and the two Keses, were doing everything they could.

As Janeway hurried through one corridor, she had seen Kes-two—at least she thought it was Kes-two—trying to calm a healthy-looking young boy who had been screaming with terror.

Janeway hoped that Torres had a better solution. One that would stop this thing before it started, completely, permanently, and effectively.

No one deserved to die like so many had, and no

one deserved to live with the memories that were forcing that young boy to scream like that.

That scream would haunt her dreams.

If, of course, she didn't resolve this.

She went through the doors of Engineering, and stopped near the warp engine. It looked so normal in here, with the clean floors and the beeping equipment. Hard to believe that outside the door, people littered the corridor because *Voyager* had run out of beds.

"There you are," Torres-two said. "We were beginning to think we had to come to you."

She looked so clean and neat, the perfect chief engineer in the middle of her domain. It was Torres who looked as if she belonged in that corridor, her uniform damp with sweat, a streak of dirt across her face, her hair tousled.

"Captain," Torres said, "you have to see this." She beckoned Janeway to the console. Torres-two stood beside her. The two Torreses started to speak—in unison.

That was too much for Janeway.

She held up a hand. "Slowly, please," she said. "And one at a time."

"Captain," they both said together and grinned at each other. Janeway recognized the giddiness. It came from solving an impossible problem, something that no one thought would ever get solved.

"All right," Janeway said. She needed to take control of this. She looked at her original chief engineer. "Lieutenant, tell me your idea."

Torres nodded and took a deep breath. Then she brought up on the screen the images of the shift, with the asteroid belts moving off to the right, and the beautiful blue planets to the left. Then on screen she overlaid the image with two lines. One line went off to the right, through the asteroids to the planets beyond, the other line to the left.

Janeway stared at the point where the two lines met near the edge of the dark sphere of humanoid bodies floating in space.

"Two things lead to the answer we've been searching for," Torres said. "The fact that all time and space, in all the universes are hooked into one universe for those short seconds, all pointing at the same exact location."

"We've located that point," Torres-two said. "And every *Voyager* can easily find it, also."

"And the second important thing is the asteroid belt itself," Torres said.

Janeway was exhausted. She knew that if she had been feeling more alert, she would have understood what Torres was saying from those two pieces of information.

"What?" Janeway asked, forcing herself to look beyond the shape of the planet made of humanoid bodies, and look to the asteroid belt. The tumbling mass of rock seemed to be nothing more than an asteroid belt created centuries before, when the planet in this orbit broke apart.

"It's bothered us both," Torres-two said, "that only these hundred or so universes have no fifth planet, while all the rest do. So we analyzed the asteroids."

Janeway felt the beginnings of the giddiness herself. She hadn't thought of that. It had been so obvious. It was such an old rule. Find the source of the difference.

The small difference.

Or the large one.

"And?" she asked.

"A space-time rift ripped the fifth planet apart about a half million years ago," Torres said.

"Not so much a rift," Torres-two corrected, "as a bubble."

"A bubble, or hole in the universes, about fifty times the size of *Voyager*."

"So why didn't this hole destroy all the other planets?" Janeway asked.

Torres shrugged. "Possibly an asteroid had hit the planet in these hundred universes, weakening the crust."

"Maybe it hit ten miles off in the other universes," Torres-two said, shrugging.

"Or not at all," Torres said. "Anyway, we know for certain that the bubble happened near, inside, or just above every planet, and has been appearing and disappearing every few thousand years for as long as we could trace."

Janeway felt her understanding grow. "The bubble is the source of extra energy that's been bothering you."

"Yes," Torres and Torres-two said in unison.

They grinned at each other again. Janeway wasn't sure she could get used to them working together so well, but she was glad that they had.

"Actually," Torres said, pointing at the screen and the lines, "the energy release of the transport is enough to cause the rift to pulse, like a heartbeat, every few hours, sending out the subspace waves and creating the connection between the universes. It's the space effect that we're dealing with here. The time effects don't seem to be noticeable."

"So that solves what caused this mess," Janeway said, but something was nagging at her. A piece that didn't make sense. "It would seem logical, though, that everything would get transported off the planet then, not just humanoids."

"Oh, no," Torres said. "You must remember the nature of the interaction."

"This is how it works," Torres-two said. "When I was on the planet, the Birsibans only had the transporter system hooked into the energy supplies, focused on humanoid forms, and what was in contact with those forms, such as clothes, baggage, that sort of thing. The power from the rift surges through the equipment and transports everyone on the planet."

"There wouldn't be a problem," Torres said, "except for the fact that in that short time the entire population is in transport, the energy flow is like a river, flowing down the timeline, to our right."

"And they get moved over one universe," Torres-two said, "like debris in a river."

"Exactly," Torres said.

That made sense to Janeway. A wild series of circumstances, all building up to the death of billions. A set of circumstances her own scientists wouldn't have been able to predict. A set that scientists in an early-warp culture like the Birsibans' wouldn't have even suspected.

"So you found the cause," Janeway said, "and that led you to the solution? You said you had one."

"Oh, yeah, we have one all right," Torres said.

"What is it?" Janeway asked. "We only have forty-five minutes until the next event."

Torres glanced at Torres-two, who nodded.

"We fly *Voyager* right into the rift," Torres said.

"All the *Voyager*s," Torres-two said.

"All at the same time," Torres said.

CHAPTER
37

Time: The ninety-second shift
Location: Our universe

JANEWAY FELT HER HEART POUNDING. SHE WAS TENSE.
This message had to get through to the other ships.
Torres had come up with a good solution, the right
solution, she was sure.

Now all they had to do was make it work.

She glanced down at her panel. They had eight
minutes until the next shift. Her bridge crew was
working hard.

Harry Kim was preparing communication.

Torres was putting the finishing touches on Janeway's message.

Paris was working on the flight plan.

Chakotay was beside her, double-checking the
numbers.

On the lower decks, Kes was helping the Doctor
get ready, in case there were problems.

Neelix was making sure that the rest of the crew
was fine.

Janeway thought of beaming a message to R'Lee

or to whomever had replaced him on the planet below. But if that R'Lee would move in the next shift, and if the plan was successful, he would be back home after the following shift.

She felt the effort would confuse him, and only serve to placate herself, to make her feel as if she had done one final thing. So instead she did nothing.

Chakotay drummed his fingers on the armrest of his command chair. She frowned. Another little difference. *Her* Chakotay would never do that.

But the Torres who had come up with the solution had come from two universes over. The strange away team had proven its worth, even if it wasn't composed of the *exact* same people she was used to.

"Captain," Torres said, as if she had known Janeway was thinking of her. "The message is compacted and ready to send."

"Excellent," Janeway said. "Mr. Kim, are you ready to receive all other messages?"

"We can handle approximately seven thousand," Kim said. "Maybe more. I hope that will be enough."

"And you'll be able to distinguish which message comes from which *Voyager?*"

"Yes, Captain," he said. "I'll use the number system you came up with."

Janeway nodded and turned back to face the screen. She knew that the captain of *Voyager twenty-four-ten* had only wanted nearby *Voyager*s to work on the problem. But Janeway just couldn't take the chance that for some small twist of fate, hers was the only *Voyager* to work out a better solution.

Of course, that assumed that the idea of flying *Voyager* right into a time rift was either not something Torres would have come up with, or something that Janeway would normally have approved. But she had listened to Torres's argument and realized that this solution was the only way to feed enough antimatter into the rift at exactly the right point. The antimatter would, in theory, destroy the rift.

Actually, it would do better than just destroy it. It would seal it, so that when the Birsibans started their transport, they wouldn't start this all over again. If it did start again, then *Voyager* would be caught in a time loop from which there would be no escape. They would be doomed over and over again to come to the rescue, try this method, fail, and start over. Time loops were the most frightening thing about time travel. She knew of a number of Federation ships that had been trapped in them. But they were only ones that had managed to somehow escape.

So sealing the rift was critical.

And when the rift was sealed, the problem of the cascading transports from one universe to the next would stop, even if Birsiba started up its transportation system.

Of course, destroying the rift would also destroy the ship, this ship with its new away team, and its creative crew. But if the action was successful, then

Janeway would still exist, with her regular crew, back in the time before they encountered the first subspace waves. She and all the other *Voyager*s in orbit over this planet would be, in effect, sacrificing themselves. But the sacrifice was necessary to save billions and billions of lives.

"Kathryn?" Chakotay said softly.

She glanced up, expecting to see the Chakotay she knew, the Chakotay she had flown with since they arrived in the Delta Quadrant. His gaze met hers, then skittered away as he seemed to realize that for a moment, he had forgotten where he was.

It seemed that the Janeway two universes over was close to her Chakotay as well.

"What, Chakotay?" Janeway asked, equally softly.

He shook his head once, as if he wanted the question forgotten.

"Chakotay?"

He opened his mouth, smiled ruefully, then said, "You looked distracted. I wondered if there was anything—"

"I was thinking of the billions of lives, Chakotay," she said. "Billions of lives that will be saved if this works."

She hesitated, then went on. "And I was thinking about the loss of this ship. And then, I was wondering if I was the only Janeway who was having these thoughts."

"It's hard to say, isn't it?" Chakotay said. His fingers continued to drum on the armrest. "We don't know how different or how similar we are to ones who bear our name in the other universes. The small differences—at what point do they become large ones?"

She smiled at him, and put her hand on his drumming fingers, stopping the one thing that made him different, in action, from the Chakotay she knew. "I think each difference is important," she said. "If I didn't, I wouldn't be sending this message during the next shift. I would assume that the others had figured it out."

"And if they have?" Chakotay asked.

"Then we lose nothing."

"And if they haven't, we stop this thing."

Janeway nodded.

"Captain, the next event is beginning," Kim said, as if she wouldn't notice the flare of light, and then the planets blooming across the screen.

Chakotay's fingers tensed beneath her hand. She moved, leaning forward, looking for the rift, and of course, not seeing it.

All those *Voyager*s.

All those Janeways.

Impossible to think, even though she had met herself, even though she had seen others who were, in essence, her, that there could be others.

And one of the others facing such horror, and still—Janeway felt a shiver of pride—still standing up to it. She could only hope that she would have done as well.

The planets faded, and the ship rocked slightly as the subspace wave passed.

"We received a message from *Voyager twenty-four-ten,*" Kim said.

"Did we receive any others, Ensign?" Janeway asked, almost holding her breath waiting for the answer.

Ensign Kim nodded, staring at his board. "More than our storage could handle," he said. "I captured at least nine thousand."

Janeway sat silently, letting the idea that over nine thousand *Voyager*s, with nine thousand Janeways and Torreses, had come up with a better solution, and all thought they might be unique enough to be the only one to think of it.

Torres looked almost stunned.

"Well," Janeway said, laughing slightly. "It's good to know we're all thinking along the same lines."

CHAPTER
38

Time: The ninety-second shift
Location: 2,410 parallel universes to the right
of ours

THE HEAT HAD GOTTEN WORSE. SWEAT DRIPPED OFF
Janeway's forehead. Her eyes were gritty with exhaustion. She leaned back in her command chair,
cursing, silently cursing those shifts.

Paris was at the helm, Paris-two beside him,
staring toward the left of the screen as if he could
still see his home universe.

Torres and Torres-two were behind her on the
bridge, along with Chakotay and Chakotay-two.
Kim was working his station, filtering through all
the messages.

Janeway wiped the sweat off her forehead with
the orange sleeve of her uniform. "First," she said,
"I want a report on the status of the survivors of
the last shift."

May as well get the bad news over with all at
once.

Torres glanced at Torres-two, then sighed. "We
managed to pack into buffers another thousand or

so, but the rest shifted out of the containment field and into the next universe."

Janeway nodded, not allowing herself to think about what those people had gone through. She didn't dare. Not if she was going to solve this. She glanced around at her crew. "I have been considering our options."

"I thought we already had a plan, Captain," Paris-two said.

"We do, Mr. Paris," Janeway said.

"Two," Paris whispered.

"Two," Janeway added, with a nod to the Paris from her ship. "But I'm not real fond of it. This plan is that we, and thousands of other *Voyagers* like us, all release antimatter into a certain position inside the time-warp rift. It will destroy our ship, but if done with every *Voyager* at the same moment, it should be enough to close the rift at a point in time *before* the shifts started. Is that correct?"

Torres and Torres-two both nodded.

Janeway had also checked their calculations. And, it seemed, so had just about every other *Voyager* in all the universes. Independently they had come up with the same plan, judging by a sampling of the thousands of messages that had flooded in during the last shift.

Her message going outward had been very, very similar to all the others coming in. She had outlined the new idea to all the ships. During the next shift she would make the decision as to what the thousands and thousands of *Voyagers* were going to do, and send it out to all of them. The weight of that decision, plus the haunting images of the billions of bodies floating in space near the ship, pressed on her like a ceiling coming down.

"It's rather like the old problem that Professor Brown used to assign at the Academy." She looked at her crew. "Did any of you study with him?"

Paris rolled his eyes. "I got him on his last semester. Just before he retired."

"You mean the ethics question?" Paris-two asked. "Is that the one?"

Janeway nodded. "I hated it. We spent two weeks on it. And it sounded so simple."

"I remember," Paris said. He made his voice sound deeper than usual. "Class, if you knew that by sacrificing one person, you could save a thousand, would you do so?"

"And everyone said, 'Of course.'"

"And then he listed the problems with it. What if you sacrificed Cochran before he invented warp drive? Or what if you sacrificed Salk before the polio vaccine? Or N'Amon before the Feeding of the Millions? Would you be saving lives or costing them?"

"We do not have time for this now," Tuvok said. "We have a case before us. It is the only solution."

Janeway smiled at him. "You didn't like Professor Brown, did you, Tuvok?"

"The scenarios weren't always logical, Captain."

"Oh, but they are, Tuvok." She pushed a strand of hair out of her face. "It is never right to sacrifice a life unnecessarily."

"You did not say in your initial question that it was unnecessary. You said—"

"I know, Mr. Tuvok," Janeway said. "And I also said Professor Brown spent two weeks on this. We don't have the time. I just feel as I did then. I wanted to make sure the sacrifice of all the *Voyagers* in this timeline is the only answer."

She felt another bead of sweat drip onto her neck. "Torres, what is the chance other *Voyagers* could come through the shift to this universe?"

Torres glanced at Torres-two, then shrugged. "I suppose they could. We can beam messages. The universes are linked during those few seconds. I'm sure other *Voyagers* could come through. They would have to dip slightly down into the upper atmosphere of the planets, but it would work."

Janeway nodded. "How many *Voyagers* would it take to set up enough containment fields to capture everyone being shifted, then transport into buffers every person captured?"

Torres shook her head, as if not believing what she was hearing. "Thirty, at least," Torres said. "Possibly more. I don't know for sure."

"More," Torres-two said.

Janeway could see her final idea breaking down before it even started to form.

Chakotay looked at her. "Are you thinking of mounting a rescue operation, Captain? Where are you thinking of placing the planet's inhabitants after we rescue them?"

"So if you count in transport time to other

nearby class-M worlds to dump the people," Torres-two said, "make that two hundred *Voyager*s, at least."

Janeway glanced at the screen. A rescue effort that would take forever.

Torres glanced at Chakotay, but before either of them could say another word, Tuvok spoke. "Captain, there are over four hundred billion bodies that form that sphere where the planet used to be. A rescue operation would not save them."

"The best way to save everyone is to stop the shifts from ever starting," Torres-two said.

"And if we're not successful?" Janeway said. "If we get destroyed and don't close the rift, then who's going to save the billions more that will shift in here?"

That simple question set them all back.

"I remember that part too," Paris said. "Do you keep killing individuals until you find the one who'll save the thousands?"

"This is not a classroom," Torres-two snapped.

"Would that it were," Tuvok said softly.

Janeway understood their reactions. They had to speak to keep their minds from being overwhelmed. Because they finally understood the magnitude of her decision.

She had to risk thousands of *Voyager*s and their crews to save billions of lives. The loss would be worth it, in many ways, if they succeeded in stopping the event before it started. All the *Voyager*s in this timeline would cease to exist, more than likely just as they were being destroyed. The timeline would reset itself to a position before any of the *Voyager*s felt the subspace waves. Those *Voyager*s in that timeline would continue on the journey home, never knowing that this timeline had ever existed.

Unlike the problem Professor Brown had set up, the thousands of *Voyager*s would not be snuffed forever. They would continue, only without this life-changing, all-important event.

And more important, the hundreds of billions of lives that had already been lost would be saved.

But if the *Voyager*s failed . . .

All the *Voyager*s would be destroyed, and there would be no one to save the billions and billions who would die horrible deaths in open space.

"Captain," Tuvok said, his voice level and calm.

Janeway nodded.

"The rescue operation you propose would not be mathematically or logically possible."

Janeway stared at her security chief. "And why not? Give me your reasoning."

"Logically, Captain, there are an unlimited number of universes with populations that, for lack of a better way of putting it, will drain to this space."

Janeway instantly grasped what he was driving at. "There aren't an unlimited number of class-M planets in this universe to put them on."

"At least not within our range," Tuvok said, nodding. "It would take two thousand, five hundred uninhabited class-M planets to take just the next year's worth of population."

"Add in travel time between systems," Torres-two said, "and you would need far more *Voyager*s than are now within reach of our communication just to maintain the operation for that length of time."

"It would not work, Captain," Tuvok said. He sounded almost apologetic.

She took a deep breath. She was out of options. Now she knew how her counterpart felt in the plasma cloud. When faced with the inevitable, the best thing to do was to walk into it, boldly.

She turned to Torres and Torres-two. "We've got over an hour before I have to send out that message to the other *Voyager*s with instructions. I want to make triple sure of these calculations, and the timing involved with discharging the antimatter."

"Yes, Captain," both Torreses said at the same time.

"What about all the Birsibans in the buffers?" Chakotay-two asked.

Janeway glanced around at the room. "They ride into the eye of the storm with us," she said. "If we succeed, they'll be home cooking breakfast and will never know what happened. If we fail . . ."

She left that word hanging in the air for a long second, then shook her head. "We're not going to fail. Now, let's get to work."

CHAPTER 39

Time: The ninety-third shift
Location: Our universe

THE TWO AND A HALF HOURS BETWEEN THE NINETY-second shift and the ninety-third were the longest two and a half hours Janeway had remembered ever spending. She had gone over the calculations for the tenth time, but came up with the same reasoning. She had even come up with a rescue idea using hundreds of *Voyager*s to capture and transport the Birsibans to new worlds. But even in spreading the rescue plan out over a hundred universes to the right of the asteroid universe, there were just not enough class-M planets within a year's travel to hold billions and billions of people from thousands of universes.

She had done an inspection of all decks, and had even inspected sickbay, much to the Doctor's dismay.

"Captain, if you have nothing to do," he had said, "I do have some cultures that need tending."

"Cultures, Doctor?"

"Bioforms," he had said. "I would love to see how they adhere to human skin."

She had left quickly.

She had even thought of returning to her reading in her ready room, but knew she wouldn't be able to concentrate.

So now she sat in her Captain's chair, waiting. Her crew was on the bridge, reviewing calculations, or just waiting with her. All four members of the away team from the other *Voyager* were on the bridge.

Chakotay was sitting beside her, drumming his fingers.

Paris was at the helm, staring at the screen as if he were seeing something new.

Kes was standing beside Neelix near the turbolift, and Torres was reviewing their plan for the thousandth time.

Janeway tried to imagine what she would do if faced with the decision the Janeway in *Voyager* twenty-four-ten was facing. Whatever the decision that captain made, there was no doubt Janeway would follow. It would be like following herself, following her own decision. And she had no doubt that in a short time she would be ordering this *Voyager* into a suicide mission, one where this *Voyager,* and this crew, would never return. If she were in that captain's shoes, that was what she would order.

There would be no other choice.

"Captain," Ensign Kim said, "we have thirty seconds until shift."

"Are you prepared to receive as many messages as possible?" She wasn't sending one out this time, but again she had to be prepared in case her thinking was different from that of the other Janeways in all the other *Voyager*s.

"Yes, Captain," Kim said.

As she turned back to the screen, the event started. The light flared, and then the planets appeared, moving away from her in two directions. Despite its terrible nature, despite all the death and destruction it had caused, this phenomenon was one of the most beautiful she had ever seen.

Like so much in the universe: It was beautiful and terrible at the same time.

And if things worked out, she would never see it again. At least not like this.

Then, as quickly as it appeared, the phenomenon vanished. The ship bounced slightly as the subspace wave hit. The crew had gotten used to that part. She could hear the bips and beeps of the control panels around her.

"We received a message from *Voyager twenty-four-ten,*" Kim said.

Janeway took a deep breath. "Did we receive any others?"

"No, Captain," Kim said, shaking his head. "Just the one."

Janeway nodded at the implications of that. Thousands of *Voyager*s and this time they were all silent, just as she had been. She turned back to face the screen. "Put the message on screen."

It was time. Time to know the solution to all of this.

Time to make the difficult choices.

A moment later, the exhausted Captain of *Voyager twenty-four-ten* appeared on the screen, and simply from the look in her eyes Janeway knew what she was going to say.

Janeway knew she would have said the same thing.

CHAPTER
40

Time: The ninety-third shift
Location: 2,410 parallel universes to the right
of ours

AS JANEWAY ENTERED THE BRIDGE FROM HER READY
room, she noticed the feeling that it was extra
crowded. Neelix stood with Kes on his right and
Kes-two on his left near the door to the conference
room. Chakotay and Chakotay-two held positions
behind the Captain's chair at the rail. Torres was at
the science station and Torres-two stood beside
Ensign Kim, helping him where needed. Paris was
at the helm, with Paris-two standing to his left,
watching. Tuvok stood at his normal station, his
hands behind his back, obviously waiting for her.

Their faces were glistening with sweat. Her original crew looked tired and battered. The away team
was beginning to lose its crispness as well.

They were waiting, just as she was.

In the last shift, the other *Voyager*s had received
her message. Billions more people had shifted into
the abyss.

Billions more had died.

"How long until the next shift, Ensign Kim?" Janeway asked.

"Eight minutes and twelve seconds," Kim said.

She nodded and glanced at the screen. The huge mass of humanoid bodies formed the dark sphere in the center of the screen. When she had recorded the last message, she had that sphere of death behind her, driving home what each *Voyager* was sacrificing itself for.

Billions of lives had been lost.

Trillions more would be if they didn't stop this strange event. She had wanted every *Voyager* captain to know that, without a doubt.

She wanted them to know what they were sacrificing themselves for.

"Lieutenant Torres," Janeway said, turning her back on the screen, "are you ready to dump the antimatter?"

Torres nodded. "I've programmed the venting into the computer. It will happen at the exact moment needed."

"Good."

The silence on the bridge seemed so unnatural. Every person watched her, waiting for her to say something. What could she say? They were all about to die and they all knew it.

It was no real comfort to think that their counterparts—their own selves—would continue in a time before this event, in a time that would never see this horror. *They* were going to cease to exist.

These people. These memories.

Janeway brushed a strand of hair from her face, and glanced at the sphere of dead bodies.

These memories weren't worth saving.

"Stand by, people. We're only going to get one chance at this. We have to do it right the first time."

No one said a word as she turned and sat down, the comfortable feel of her command chair wrapping around her. On the screen was the mass of dead, floating in the cold of space. If they could close this rift at the right moment in time, all those deaths would never occur.

That would be worth every sacrifice.

Every *Voyager*.

The silence stretched on until finally Ensign Kim said, "We have one minute, Captain."

"Mr. Paris," Janeway said, "move us into position."

Slowly the image of the mass of dead grew in size until she could almost see individual bodies.

Almost.

"Ten seconds," Kim said. His voice was clearly strained and Janeway could tell he was struggling to hold on. But she had no doubt he would make it. He had a heart of steel.

"Are you ready, Lieutenant Torres?" Janeway asked.

"Ready, Captain," Torres said.

"Five," Kim said, starting the countdown.

Janeway's gaze met Chakotay's. He nodded at her.

"Four."

Then she turned back to the screen. The sphere of dead bodies faced her, gray and dark and silent.

"Three."

"Take us in, Mr. Paris," Janeway said, feeling much calmer than she had just moments before.

"Two."

"Aye, Captain," Paris said.

"One."

Janeway gripped her armrests. Her crew looked straight ahead, as she did, facing death with all the strength and courage they had.

Then Mr. Kim said the word she had come to dread:

"Shift."

CHAPTER
41

Time: The ninety-fourth shift
Location: Our universe

"EIGHT MINUTES UNTIL THE SHIFT, CAPTAIN," KIM
said. He was standing at his console, working it as
quickly as his fingers could move. Janeway glanced
at him over her own science console. She had
checked and rechecked the figures, partly because
she needed something to do, so that she wouldn't
dwell on what was going to happen next.

Still, she surfaced every time Kim continued the
countdown. Eight minutes left.

Eight minutes until this *Voyager,* all of these
Voyagers, ceased to exist.

She only hoped they would know if they succeeded or not. The last thing she wanted was to be
destroyed before they knew whether or not they
had sealed the space-time rift.

Her entire crew, including its four newest members, seemed to be using work as a way of dealing
with the next few minutes. The only one who

wasn't was Neelix. He was standing near the turbolift, watching Kes. Only she wasn't the Kes he
knew. Janeway could see the wistfulness on his
face.

Sometimes a person couldn't be near the ones
they were closest to at the end. She had Tuvok, who
had been her friend for a long, long time, but Mark
was long gone, and Chakotay . . .

She shook her head and stared down at the
console. Instead of seeing the numbers, she remembered the message that had come through the last
rift.

The message from *Voyager twenty-four-ten* had
been sobering and very much to the point. The
captain of that *Voyager* had stood with the images
of billions of dead floating in space behind her,
outlining exactly what each *Voyager* needed to do.

"I'm sure you all understand the difficulties we
face," that Janeway had said. "I am comforted by
the fact that we have reached the solution together,
and that we all agree." She had smiled then. "I will
see you in the rift."

And then her image had faded.

Her image had faded.

As all of theirs would.

Fade.

Cease to exist.

Janeway sighed, and looked at the figures before
her for the final time. Along with the verbal message had come all the exact calculations. Janeway
and Torres had spent an hour after the message
going over every calculation three times. The num-

bers were right. Enough antimatter dumped at exactly the correct location in the rift would seal the rift at a point in time *before* the shifts started.

That was important. When Paris had first heard of this, he had thought that it would all be in vain.

"With us gone," he had said, "what's to stop the Birsibans from using their transportation systems?"

"Nothing," Torres had answered.

"Then this will be a fruitless exercise," Paris said.

Torres had given him a measuring look. To Janeway's surprise, and pleasure, Torres hadn't insulted him. "Tom," she said, "it's not the transportation system that causes the problem. It's the rift. It's fueling this interuniversal shift. When the rift is sealed, the Birsibans can transport to their hearts' delight, and end up in other places on their planet, not in other universes."

"Oh," Paris had said, flushing. "Missed that."

And that was the most important point. If they sealed the rift, they stopped the problem.

Forever.

Every *Voyager* would be destroyed within five seconds after venting the antimatter as they all came together, but that would make no difference to the overall outcome since this timeline would, at the sealing of the rift, cease to exist. Janeway and Torres had even spent ten minutes arguing whether all the *Voyager*s from all the universes would actually collide, or if they would all cease to exist first. Either way it didn't matter.

She and all the other Janeways on all the other *Voyager*s agreed.

This timeline had to end.

And to do that, all the *Voyager*s were going to be destroyed in one massive operation.

"We have five minutes, Captain," Ensign Kim said.

Janeway nodded. Did she need to say anything? To the crew? Or those on the bridge?

She glanced at them. At all of them. The new Torres had proven as effective as the other Torres, two universes away. Paris had managed the helm just fine. And this Kes was just as compassionate.

Then why, why did she wish for the others?

Especially Chakotay. She wanted to see his rueful smile, his dark eyes, to touch his hand one last time.

She looked at Tuvok. He nodded to her formally, then returned his attention to his console.

She smiled. No words were necessary between them.

No words could encompass what they all faced. The crew, every one of them, had seen the images of those billions of bodies floating in space. She had no doubt that every crew member could imagine what it would be like to be at home one moment, enjoying a sunny afternoon, the next moment to suddenly find themselves in space, dying.

No, there was no need for her to say anything to the crew. They would all do their jobs during the last few minutes, and face the end with dignity.

She stared at the beautiful planet on the main screen. It seemed so peaceful. Paris said it was.

She hoped it would be again.

She hoped the right R'Lee would have the right daughter with the green—or was it brown?—eyes. That small detail was lost to the whims of her memory.

The small detail that had brought the ship to this planet in the first place.

She smiled. She hoped the Birsibans would enjoy their new transportation system, and move on to the next stage of their existence.

She hoped they would all come back to their homes, to their lives, to face a normal existence that would end in the normal way, whatever that was for Birsibans.

Not a sudden, hideous death in the vacuum of space.

"Two minutes, Captain," Ensign Kim said.

Time for her to take action.

She swallowed. Her mouth was dry. She looked at Torres, who was also staring at the screen.

"Lieutenant," Janeway said, "are you ready to vent the antimatter?"

"The target is programmed into the computer and ready to go," Torres said. Her eyes were bright and she looked very Klingon. Janeway could almost hear in each word the old Klingon affirmation: *This is a good day to die.*

"I even performed a backup maneuver," Torres said, "so that I can do the whole thing manually if I have to."

"Excellent, Lieutenant," Janeway said. She looked at the helm. "Ready to fly us into the rift, Mr. Paris?"

"As ready as I'll ever be," he said, without turning to her.

She glanced once at Chakotay. He did smile at her. Ruefully, just as the other Chakotay would have. But his fingers drummed on the armrest, and this time she let them.

Then she turned back to face the viewscreen, her hands gripping the sides of her command chair. In her mind, the image of the billions of dead lay over the beauty of the planet like a shadow of a storm cloud on a sunny day.

She took a deep breath.

"Captain, we have twenty seconds," Kim said.

Silence filled the bridge. Silence thicker than any silence Janeway had ever heard. Her entire crew was poised and ready.

"Ten seconds," Kim said.

"Take us into position, Mr. Paris," Janeway ordered.

"Breaking orbit," Paris said.

The planet grew on the screen in front of them. They were committed.

They could not turn back.

"Five seconds," Kim said.

She almost wished she had given that last speech.

"Four."

Paris bent over the helm, his gaze on the planet before him.

"Three."

Chakotay's fingers stopped drumming. She resisted the urge to touch his hand.

"Two."

Out of the corner of her eye, she saw Neelix walk toward Kes.

"One."

The planet grew larger than she had ever seen it.

"Shift."

In front of them, the planet shimmered as the whiteness spread outward. Then suddenly the other planets were there, moving off into the distance in two directions.

But this time the angle was different. Janeway noted with a smile that all the other *Voyager*s were in the same position as hers, just above the planet's atmosphere, and moving down.

"Take us into the rift, Mr. Paris," Janeway ordered as *Voyager* seemed to accelerate directly at the surface of the planet.

"Entering the rift, now!" Kim shouted.

Just as suddenly as the multiple planets had appeared, they vanished, replaced by a place like nothing Janeway had ever seen before.

It was as if *Voyager* were immersed in a clear, almost bluish fluid, that shimmered and swirled like the clear water of a mountain stream. Almost peaceful, like floating under water in a clear pool. But here there were no sides, no bottom, no surface.

Just clear, blue fluid.

Thousands and thousands of *Voyager*s in a line disappeared off into the distance in two directions.

All the *Voyager*s were flying down and toward each other, heading toward the exact same point. Janeway felt she could almost reach out and touch the *Voyager* closest to them on either side.

She knew all the other captains had to be feeling the same.

On the ship to her right, her original away team watched this phenomenon.

The ship to the left was where the away team on her bridge had come from.

They were so close, almost as if a line could be tossed between them.

And they were getting closer.

And closer.

Voyager rocked slightly.

"Hold course," Janeway ordered. She could see Paris sweating, his fingers flying over the board in front of him as he fought to keep the ship on course for its last flight. How many thousands, maybe millions, of other Parises were doing the exact same thing on other *Voyager*s?

"Venting antimatter now!" Torres shouted.

On screen, in either direction, Janeway saw thousands of red streams of antimatter cut through the bluish fluid of the rift toward a point directly in front of all of them.

The streams all shot forward like red laser fire, merging into one large stream at one exact place, lighting the bluish fluid with the red of a spectacular sunset.

Janeway watched in awe. It seemed as if, in front of them, a new star had been born. And the birthplace was right at the one point where all the universes met.

"Direct hit!" Torres shouted.

"From all the *Voyager*s," Tuvok added.

"Impact in two seconds!" Kim shouted.

The bright reds and oranges of the antimatter explosions surrounded them, bathing the bridge in a blood red.

The edges of the other *Voyager*s on either side of them seemed to fill the viewscreen like massive red walls closing in, tighter and tighter.

Thousands, maybe millions, of *Voyager*s were all converging on the exact same point in time and space.

In a moment, millions of *Voyager*s would all compact down into a space big enough for only one.

It would be a collision the size of which had never been seen in all of human history. Maybe even the history of the Alpha Quadrant.

Janeway couldn't speak for the Delta Quadrant.

She just wished there were a way to watch this collision from the outside.

"The rift is sealed!" Torres shouted, her voice jubilant.

Two nearby *Voyager*s hit *Voyager*.

"We're crashing," Kim said, but his words were drowned out by a small cheer that the crew let out in unison as a response to Torres's words.

The rift was sealed.

The red from the antimatter explosion disappeared, returning the ship to the blue of the rift.

Janeway smiled to herself as she held onto her seat and the ship rocked on its way to destruction.

They had succeeded.

She felt a quiet joy.

The billions of deaths would never happen.

The universe had been reset.

That was her last thought—all of the Janeways' last thought—as thousands, maybe millions of *Voyager*s smashed down into a single point.

Then the ships faded and vanished, as if they had never been.

And inside the sealed space-time rift near the planet Birsiba, they never had.

EPILOGUE

Time: Normal
Location: Our universe

Captain Kathryn Janeway glanced up from the screen of her book padd at the stars out the viewports of the ready room. The soft beep of an incoming call had jarred her out of a fictional early nineteenth-century world back into the twenty-fourth century.

She sighed and glanced back at the padd. She had tired of reading about gloomy governesses in remote mansions on the moors, and was sampling a period piece with a different flavor, a comedy of manners set during the British Regency, Earthdate 1816, though written a century later. In her off-duty hours she enjoyed reading about stratified, rigid societies where people behaved according to outmoded codes.

Not that she had many off-duty hours these days. Off-duty minutes seemed more like it. The warp engines had failed a week before, and she and Lieutenant Torres had been putting in long hours getting them back on-line. Then a personnel crisis had erupted among the junior engineering staff. Normally, she would have let B'Elanna handle it, but Klingons—even half-Klingons—had notoriously foul moods when they were sleep-deprived. Chakotay had tried to settle it, but his usual low-key style had failed. Janeway had stepped in, using the last of her energy and all of her diplomatic skills. The crisis had passed, but it had taken her reserves with it.

Both Chakotay and Tuvok had hinted that she needed rest. This afternoon, she took their advice, but she couldn't bring herself to take the entire afternoon off. She had too much work to catch up on. She didn't have time for her favorite holodeck program, so she had picked up an old novel instead.

She liked books. A real book could be read in snatches, seconds of escape and relaxation, instead of an afternoon's worth. Sometimes seconds were all she had.

But in those seconds, she could disappear into a good book. And this book was good.

With another sigh she pushed it aside for the moment and hit her comm link. "Yes?"

"Captain?" Kes's voice came through hesitantly. "I'm sorry to disturb you, but may I have a moment?"

"Of course," Janeway said. "Come in."

She dipped back into her book for another moment, then she heard the pneumatic hiss of the doors. Kes came in, and the doors closed behind her.

Kes's wide eyes had deep circles under them, and a frown creased her forehead. Yet, in typical Kes fashion, she remained calm. She stopped in front of Janeway, hands clasped behind her back.

Janeway set her padd aside.

"I'm sorry to bother you," Kes said.

Janeway smiled and leaned back. "It's all right. Would you like a seat?"

Kes shook her head. She seemed almost embarrassed. She glanced at the flowers she had brought to the ready room the day before. "They'll need changing soon."

"They're fine," Janeway said. "What brings you here?"

"It's silly," Kes said. "If there was a problem, you wouldn't be here."

Now she had caught Janeway's interest. "A problem?"

"I could have sworn we received a distress call," Kes said. "But no one is acting as if we had."

"No one's informed me of any distress call," Janeway said, then frowned. Tuvok and Chakotay had been almost too protective of late. Did they think they would investigate a distress call's validity before contacting her? "But let me check."

Kes nodded once, uncomfortably, as if she weren't quite certain of what was happening. And it did seem odd. Kes was usually in sickbay, one of the last places to hear of a distress call.

Still, Janeway punched her comm link. "Commander?"

"Go ahead, Captain," Chakotay's voice came back clear and firm.

"Did we just receive a distress call of any nature?"

"No, Captain," Chakotay said. "Is there something wrong?"

"No, Commander. Everything is fine here," Janeway said and signed off.

She turned back to Kes and leaned forward slightly. "Nothing. What did you feel?"

Kes looked off into the distance, then shook her head slowly. "I'm not sure, Captain. It just seemed for a moment that something had happened. Something big. Something important. But now the feeling has passed."

Janeway had learned to respect Kes's instincts. "Is it something we need to follow up on?"

Kes still had the distant look in her eyes, as if she were consulting the memory of the feeling that had brought her to the ready room. "No, Captain. I think everything is all right."

"Well," Janeway said, "if you feel it again, don't hesitate to let me know. I've come to trust these feelings of yours."

Kes nodded and smiled. "Thank you, Captain."

With that she turned and left. Janeway stared after her for a moment, wondering what had triggered Kes's feeling.

She would never know.

She picked up her padd and resumed the novel, happy to have the time alone.

And an entire afternoon to relax.

STAR TREK®
THE NEXT GENERATION™
THE
CONTINUING
MISSION

A TENTH ANNIVERSARY TRIBUTE

◆The definitive commemorative album for
one of Star Trek's most beloved shows.

◆Featuring more than 750 photos
and illustrations.

JUDITH AND GARFIELD REEVES-STEVENS
INTRODUCTION BY RICK BERMAN
AFTERWORD BY ROBERT JUSTMAN

Available in Hardcover
From Pocket Books

POCKET
BOOKS

Coming Next Month from Pocket Books

STARFLEET ACADEMY®

The Best and the Brightest
by
Susan Wright

**Please turn the page for an excerpt from
Starfleet Academy:**
The Best and the Brightest

JAYME WAS RIGHT—no one paid any attention to three orange-clad workers opening the access port in the alleyway. Kids were running past, women were hanging clothes out overhead, and antigrav carts laden with warehouse goods or fresh produce trundled by on both sides.

Closing the portal overhead, they stood in a rounded dirt-floor chamber similar to the one shown on the media broadcasts—where Data's head was found. Titus felt a sinking feeling, wondering if all the caverns had been reconditioned by the workforces over the years.

"This way," he ordered, keeping his worries to himself. At the rear of the chamber was a long ladder leading down. Here the walls were more jagged and the black pit was too deep to be illuminated by their hand lights. Titus began to feel a little better. "Down we go!"

"Wait," Jayme said, unslinging her pack. "We have to put these on."

She held out the white jet-boots issued by Starfleet.

Titus took one look and groaned. "We don't need those!"

"I'm not going without safety gear," Jayme insisted. "And I'm not going to let you two go, either. This is supposed to be fun, not life-threatening." She glanced down into the shaft. "And those rungs look slimy."

Bobbie Ray checked the two pairs she set out for them. "You brought my size!"

Jayme slipped her white boots on and tightened the straps. With a little puff of dust, she activated the jets and lifted a few inches off the ground. "Good for thirty hours use."

Bobbie Ray buckled his boots on and was soon lifting himself up to the ceiling. "Maybe we should skip the ladder and go down this way."

"Maybe you want to give up now and go back to the Quad!" Titus retorted. "What's the use of exploring if you might as well be in a holodeck?"

Both of them hovered silently, staring down at him. After a few moments, Titus flung up his hands. "Have it your way, then! But we only use the boots in an emergency or I'm quitting right now."

Jayme sank back down to the ground. "That's why I brought the jet-boots. For emergencies."

Titus waited until Bobbie Ray also slowly floated down before jerking on his jet-boots and tightening them in place. "*I* think if you can't manage to hang on to a ladder, then you get what you deserve."

Bobbie Ray laughed. "Then you go first, fearless leader."

Titus had the satisfaction of hearing the Rex's laughter abruptly end as they started down the ladder. For most humanoids, any sort of vertical drop offered a test of nerves. Especially when you couldn't see the bottom.

The light at the opening dwindled as they descended. He skipped the side tunnel that went in the direction of the Presidio and Starfleet Academy, choosing to go as deep as they could. The fracture widened at the bottom, becoming more rugged and raw. They went through a steeply inclined crack, into an underground canyon that stretched as far across as the Assembly Hall. A stream had eroded the bottom into a gorge, and they had to edge along the wall, brushing their hands against the slippery, calcified coating on the rocks. Titus could imagine the tremendous force of earthquakes breaking open the crust around the San Andreas Fault, leaving behind a network of caverns and crushed rock.

Titus took them up a high talus mound and into the next cavern, where flowstone coated the cave fill, narrowing the volume of the void. This cavern was filled with fallen ceiling blocks and the stalactites had been broken off short by earth tremors. Additional seepage gave them an unusually fat, short appearance.

They retreated to the shaft. Though the ladder left off, the shaft continued down. Titus uncoiled the rope he had brought and hooked them into it. The other two followed him without a word of complaint.

It wasn't far to the bottom, where another inclined tunnel led them east again, following the path of the caverns overhead. Water coated the walls, and after tramping carefully through the tunnel, Titus noticed a fissure overhead only because he was looking for it. Just as he suspected, once they had muscled their way up to the top of the shaft, they were in another large cavern, in line with the other two they had passed through.

"It was cut off from the last cavern by the talus mound," Titus said nonchalantly, pleased that he had guessed correctly.

They had to go through a jog in the shaft to get into the cavern, and they were slightly elevated above the floor. Jumping down, Titus felt the loose rock shift and slip under his feet. Jayme actually went down on her hands and knees, unable to keep her balance, while Bobbie Ray hung on to the stone lip they had just jumped over, staring up open-mouthed at the dramatic long, hanging ceiling that dripped continuously, the fat drops sparkling like rainbow stars under their hand lights.

"Look up here!" Jayme called, halfway up the gentle slope of the talus incline. "I think the ceiling fell in back here."

"It looks like the roof sank until it ran into the ground," Bobbie Ray agreed, swatting at the elusive, fat drops that bombed them from above.

They climbed the shifting slope to the point where the ground and ceiling met. Rounded debris constantly moved under their hands and knees. Titus examined some of the bits and was surprised to see elongated pieces as well as the more traditional "pearls."

"Why aren't there any stalactites in this cavern?" Jayme asked, standing in the last possible space at the upper end. A dense curtain of drops speckled the air in front of them.

"If there's too much water, there's no time for the sediment to form between each drop," Titus explained.

"That's what makes the cave pearls—the sediment forms as they're polished and agitated by the water."

"I think they're beautiful," Jayme said, gathering a few in her hand.

Titus squatted down next to her in a relatively drip-free zone. He aimed his tricorder at one of the elongated pearls. "This is bone! Human bone!"

Bobbie Ray immediately dropped his pearls, absently rubbing his hands on his coveralls as he looked at the tricorder readings. "You're right. They're ancient!"

Jayme was also hanging over his arm, trying to see. "Give me a second," he ordered, keying in the commands. "Somewhere between twelve and fifteen thousand years old!"

"That's when humans first moved onto this continent," Jayme breathed, gently cupping her pearls in her palms. "They must have used these caves as shelter or storage. This is amazing!"

Titus hardly had a chance to savor their find before Bobbie Ray muttered, "Uh-oh! I think we've got trouble."

The Rex was staring back at the hole they had climbed up. Water was welling up and pouring over the low lip that held back the piles of cave pearls. It made a rushing sound as it disappeared into the ground.

"What's happening?!" Bobbie Ray cried in true panic. "How are we going to get out?"

Jayme dipped her fingers in the water and stuck them in her mouth. "Salty. That's what I was afraid of. The tide must be rising."

They both turned to look at Titus, mutely demanding that he do something. He knew he probably looked as panicked as Bobbie Ray. "The tide?"

"Yes, the tide's coming in," Jayme repeated, frantically scrambling through the cave pearls to the wall, examining it with her hand light. "I don't see a high-water mark anywhere. Could it . . . Is it possible . . ."

"You mean this whole cave gets filled with water?" Bobbie Ray asked in a high voice.

Titus could only shake his head. "I don't know! We don't have oceans on Antaranan!"

"What!" Jayme shrieked. "You brought us in here and you didn't know what you were doing?"

"I'm going in," Titus said, suddenly feeling much calmer, knowing that he had to take control. He'd gotten them into this mess.

"You'll drown!" Jayme cried out. "That tunnel we came down—it's lower than this cave. It must be filled with water too!"

Titus swallowed, remembering how long the tunnel was. "We may not have oceans on Antaranan, but that doesn't mean we didn't have water. I'm a good swimmer."

"I'm not!" Bobbie Ray wailed, trying to shake the water from the fur on his hands. He was shivering and wet through.

"Get up to the top," Titus ordered. "I'll be back with help."

The other two cadets reluctantly retreated as he flung gear from his pouch—water flask, extra rope—leaving only the necessities with enough room left to wedge his jet-boots in.

Standing hip deep in the hole, wincing from the biting cold water, he glanced back up at the cadets. "Hang tight!"

They didn't look reassured.

Taking a deep breath, he ducked under the water. Immediately he knew it wouldn't work. The surge of water welling up carried him back to the surface.

As he broke into the air again, he was saying, "All right! It's all right! I've got an idea."

He quickly removed the jet-boots from his pouch and strapped them on. Water was nearing his waist now. He didn't care if it killed him, he wasn't going to give up this time.

Diving down headfirst, he turned on the boots. The jets churned the water and almost drove him into the rock wall, but he eased off the power and used his hands to guide him around the jag in the tunnel. Underwater, even with the hand light he could hardly see, so he groped his way down, feeling the scrape of rocks against his coveralls as the boots propelled him through the water.

Everything was getting dark and hazy, and his chest seemed ready to burst. Titus wasn't sure he was going to make it to the vertical shaft.

* * *

Jayme felt sorry for Bobbie Ray, huddled next to her at the top of the talus slope. "Maybe it won't reach this far," she offered.

Bobbie Ray was wiping at his fur with the fleshy palm of one hand, smoothing and smoothing it, pressing all the water out. Then he would twitch and shake, making the damp hair stand out again. Then he would pick another patch and begin the whole process over again. It seemed more like a nervous reaction than an effort to dry himself.

"Do you think he drowned yet?" Bobbie Ray asked, unable to meet her eyes.

"Umm," she murmured. "By now, he either drowned or got out alive."

"Are you going to try it?" Bobbie Ray asked.

Jayme wasn't aware that her calculating glances at the hole had been that obvious. "I'll try it before I drown in here."

Bobbie Ray went back to stroking his fur, concentrating on every swipe.

"I'll help you," she assured him.

"That won't do any good. I could barely pass the Starfleet swimming requirements. And you don't know how hard that was for me."

Jayme silently patted his knee. She wasn't sure she could make it, but every bit of her mind and body was focused on that hole, ready to dive through the water and turn on her jet-boots just like Titus. Even if it did kill her. Because that was better than sitting here until the water rose up around her chin.

"I just wish I knew if he made it," she murmured.

"Wait a few more minutes. Maybe he'll come back."

They both stared at the hole.

The shaft was full of water too. Titus desperately revved the boots, aiming straight up, his hand clenched on the control so tightly that even if he drowned he knew he would surface.

When he thought he was passing out, he broke into air. The shower of water that rose with him, and his surge in speed left him gasping and laughing and, when he finally could, crying out in relief. Arrowing up, he raised both arms, trying to pick up more speed, thinking about Jayme and Bobbie Ray back in that death trap.

He was going so fast that the opening approached before he realized it. Braking, he hit the ceiling and bounced down, managing to twist in midair in order to land on the floor of the access entrance.

Still panting and gasping, almost hysterical with his near miss, he rolled over in the dirt, trying to wipe the muddy dust that settled on his face and eyes. When he could finally see, Starsa, Moll Enor and Nev Reoh were several meters away, standing in the access room staring at him.

"What happened to you!" Moll Enor demanded.

"What are you doing here?" Titus said at the same time.

Starsa raised one hand slightly, blinking in amazement at his dramatic appearance. "I listened outside your door the other night, and I heard you planning to come down to the caves without me—"

"You what!" Titus interrupted, wishing he could box her ears. "I should report you—"

"I saw the hole filling with water," Starsa retorted, "and my tricorder said you were down there."

"We beamed over because we were afraid you were in trouble," Moll Enor added.

"We are!" Titus forgot about Starsa's gross invasion of privacy—just one of many—seeing only the heavy packs Nev Reoh was sitting on. "Jayme and Bobbie Ray are trapped in a cavern down below. The tide's coming in and it's filling the tunnels!"

Look for STAR TREK Fiction from Pocket Books

Star Trek®: The Original Series

Star Trek: The Next Generation®

Star Trek: Deep Space Nine®

Star Trek: Voyager®

Flashback • Diane Carey
Mosaic • Jeri Taylor

Star Trek®: New Frontier

Star Trek®: Day of Honor